Poetry Heroes

A Tribute

Edited By Andy Porter

First published in Great Britain in 2024 by:

YoungWriters®
Est. 1991

Young Writers
Remus House
Coltsfoot Drive
Peterborough
PE2 9BF
Telephone: 01733 890066
Website: www.youngwriters.co.uk

All Rights Reserved
Book Design by Ashley Janson
© Copyright Contributors 2024
Softback ISBN 978-1-83565-883-3
Printed and bound in the UK by BookPrintingUK
Website: www.bookprintinguk.com
YB0610D

Foreword

Our latest competition, Poetry Heroes, focuses on the people that these young poets look up to. This anthology is an impressive snapshot of the inventive, original and skilful writing of young people today, expressing their appreciation for the people that mean the most to them.

Here at Young Writers our aim is to encourage creativity in children and to inspire a love of the written word, so it's great to get such an amazing response, with some absolutely fantastic poems. It's important to focus on and celebrate others and this competition allowed these poets to write about who and what inspires them. The result is a collection of thoughtful and moving poems in a variety of poetic styles that also showcase their creativity and writing ability. Seeing their work in print will encourage them to keep writing as they grow and become our poets of tomorrow.

I'd like to congratulate all the young poets in this anthology, it's a wonderful achievement and I hope this inspires you to continue with your creative writing.

Contents

Independent Entrants

Arabella Acklam (10)	1
Annabelle Eromosele (8)	2
Gracie Roberts (16)	6
Zafreen Chowdhury (15)	9
Claire Olajide (14)	10
Pegi Barnes (9)	13
Harry Gu (9)	14
Immy Oliver (9)	17
Francesca Budnyj (18)	18
Lazzaro Pasquariello (13)	21
Ayan Sinha (15)	22
Laura Orosz (14)	25
Joy Green (12)	26
Angel Jacobs (14)	28
Rebecca Yang (8) & Michelle Do (8)	30
Akshara Madur (13)	32
Lily Passeron (13)	34
Pone-Pone Htet (11)	37
Charlie Kirk (9)	38
James Davenport (10)	41
Ella Nicholls (8)	42
Aisha Desai	45
Hafsa Muhammad Nusair (13)	46
Marcela Demcak (13)	48
Rashida Khan (15)	50
Debbie Wong (9)	52
Adithi Madur (13)	54
Shruthi Dushyanthan (12)	56
Bobby Grigore (16)	58
Dhruti Shreekumar (10)	60
Malaika Khan (15)	62
Amaarah Hussain (12)	64
Eleanor Price (15)	66
Amirah Shafii (12)	68
Zineddine Chennoufi (12)	70
Aydin Nasif (10)	72
Danielle Teknikio (13)	74
Emelia Craddock (12)	76
Noor-Ul-Huda Mughal (12)	78
Veya Berg (10)	80
Beata Kalthi (11)	82
Eva Raghavendra (10)	84
Frida Rocha (16)	86
Maya Beane (7)	88
Bayley Layton (13)	90
Haneefah Ali (12)	92
Benjamin Doeteh (17)	94
Aisha-Eniola Tandjigora (9)	95
Chikaima Onyenyionwu (10)	96
Attalia Schultz-Nazim (10)	97
Zuzanna Kalek (15)	98
Vera Krauchuk-Muzhiv (12)	99
Ishpel Williams (14)	100
Pranav Shake (11)	102
Arabella Pasquariello (10)	103
Bella Hayes (13)	104
Imaan Rahman (12)	105
Kai Beverton (15)	106
Eleanor Lancaster (15)	107
Isra Butt (11)	108
Mimi Clarke (14)	109
Ruby Cobb (12)	110
Aiden Wilson (12)	112
Rameen Ali (14)	114
Aaditri Manjunath (10)	115
Jude Meeks (13)	116
Oluwamomi Elugbaju (12)	117
Abeerah Meher Saleem (12)	118

David Chibundu Umensofor (9)	119	Juliet Else (11)	166
Eve Crutchley (12)	120	Poppy Orr (17)	167
Eleanor Downey (12)	121	Meghana Meda (14)	168
Bright Adebowale (13)	122	Luca Faulkner (13)	169
Joel Davies (17)	123	Olivia Hollinworth (8)	170
Mohammed Lehry (14)	124	Tia Hurt-Field (14)	171
Megan Munro (13)	125	Stella Rajkumar (14)	172
Reuben Mustoe (12)	126	Ayan Varma (9)	173
Maya Kasmani (9)	127	James Short (14)	174
Lily Simpson (12)	128	Daniel Kiley (9)	175
Matilda Brown (14)	130	Adhisaya Nagulenthiran (10)	176
Rosalind Thornhill-King (12)	132	Tiarna Forbes (15)	177
Jude Quail (13)	133	Khudeeja Begum (18)	178
Gurneet Singh (13)	134	Lily Parkin (13)	179
Alisha Ahmed (10)	135	Caroline Deng (9)	180
Connie Edwards (12)	136	Daisy Stockford (11)	181
Emily Barrett (11)	137	Elliott Street (9)	182
Tahmeed Rahman (13)	138	Maisy Williams (12)	183
Joyleen Shasha (8)	139	Lydia Joy (12)	184
Cotty Vicary (10)	140	Alae Habbal (10)	185
Zahara Lewis-Coombs (9)	141	Logan Jones (13)	186
Alicia Jones (14)	142	Sofia Dingsdale-Rasburn (10)	187
Hansikaa Mallieswaran (9)	143	Ariana Iqbal (7)	188
Marzia Husseini (11)	144	Ezinne Ronami Turner (8)	189
Macauley Heath Ward (14)	146	Shayna Pancholi (10)	190
Zea Windett (12)	147	Allie Wolloff (15)	191
Eoghan Bradley (12)	148	Shaswi Agrawal (12)	192
Eva Richards (10)	149	Faith Varndell (13)	193
Jade Owen (14)	150	Kaylen Pancholi (7)	194
Khloe Ndjoli (14)	151	Nandini Singh (11)	195
Brodie Terry (16)	152	Victor Umahi Ndiwe (11)	196
Charlie Watson (14)	153	Hateem Safdar (12)	197
Khadija Razaq (7)	154	Emily Rowlands (13)	198
Grace Gavin-Sommerville (14)	155	Enzo Tavaglione (6)	199
Megi Gancheva (15)	156	Amelia Wagstaff (12)	200
Temilayo Adegbaju (11)	157	Matylda Firth (12)	201
Anjolaoluwa Deborah Ojeyemi (11)	158	Amber Da Silva Lima (12)	202
Tyler Roberts (13)	159	Abheer Shetty (11)	203
Hayley Aurora Yarwood (8)	160	Lydia Difford (11)	204
Evie Jones (11)	161	Khadija Rehman (10)	205
Daniella Appiah (15)	162	Ellie Hewitt (15)	206
Yusra Taj (16)	163	Grace Ilupeju (10)	207
Ailis Mayfield (13)	164	Mrinal Shrestha (11)	208

Cora O'Hagan (13)	209
Vida Lukas (15)	210
Emma Williams (12)	211
Henry Fattorusso (9)	212
Anna Lean (13)	213
Amy Best (12)	214
Gracey-Ellen Bestwick (11)	215
Musa Alam (6)	216
Oliver Heap (13)	217
Avneet Kaur (8)	218
Myriam Amin (8)	219
Charly Hecox (10)	220
Yousuf Shah (8)	221
Blossom Fattorusso (6)	222
Joy Ilupeju (8)	223
Hareer Akram (9)	224
Eshaal Zahid (10)	225
Maggie Egerton (7)	226
Finley Stott (13)	227
Josie Robertson (9)	228
Aycha Ben-Saïd (9)	229
Ewan Jones (17)	230
Robin Brown (8)	231
Georgina Summers (12)	232
Vivienne Evette Georgieva (10)	233
Morgan McVicar (13)	234
Amelie Isenburg Daw (12)	235
Rereloluwa Solaru (8)	236
Alfie Webbern (13)	237
Olivia Dodimead (9)	238
Nicole Bujor (9)	239
Tanvi Mishra (6)	240
Heidi Colbert (10)	241
Joshua Marcou (12)	242
Amina Ali (5)	243
Glen McBain (15)	244

The Poems

Winning Whitehill

Once I forgot the words to our song,
Once I got my spelling words wrong,
Once in PE, I fell on my face,
Once my juice leaked all over the place.

I can add and subtract and move a decimal point,
Three-minute sessions to practise times tables,
I got so good I became a rock legend!

From nursery to Year Four I have loved every teacher,
Not only did they teach me,
They encouraged me to be a great leader.

At Whitehill the staff are amazing,
We were encouraged to learn even when we were isolating.

Friendships are important, to help us grow and laugh,
Practising a silly dance that really makes us laugh.

Adventure playground is for giggles and screams,
A place to feel the gentle breeze,
A place to share with my friends,
A safe place to do whatever I please.

Our school anthem is World in Union,
And at our school, there is a winner in us all.
We are the children of Whitehill,
And we are responsible, respectful and always ready.

Arabella Acklam (10)

My Dad, My Hero

This is my dad, and he is a very hardworking man.
He has a job as a manager, and sometimes,
When he picks me up, he buys some food for me.
Some days, he works at home to spend time with me.
He has a wife, and they are both from Africa.
His wife has two jobs. She is very industrious.
However, she spends a lot of time with me
And my brother when she is around.
Both my dad and mum are very hardworking.
They both ensure that whatever I request is given to me.

My dad's favourite colour is blue;
On Sundays, he goes to church to worship God and pray.
On Saturdays, he stays home with our little brother,
Who is six years old,
And my dad is fifty-one years old.
My dad loves singing, so he is a singer,
And on the holidays, he takes me to many places
Around the world, such as
Southend, Blackpool, France and Turkey.
Sometimes, he takes us to the park on sunny days,
But sometimes, when I ask to go to the park,
He says no because it is not sunny,
And he doesn't want me to get a cold.

And on Sundays, I go to a gymnastics club,
And my dad drives me to the place
Where I do my gymnastics.
Sometimes, when I finish my club,
I go swimming, go home, brush my teeth, and go to bed.
My dad prays and then tucks me into bed.

The next day, my dad wakes me up at 6:30am
To get ready for my sister's morning singing at 8:25am.
When we are ready, my dad drives us
To school for my sister to sing, and then I wait outside
And then when it is 8:45, I go inside for my schoolwork.
My mum picks me up every other day except Wednesday
Because my dad picks me up instead
Because he has to go to work on all of the other days,
But on Wednesday, he works at home.
My dad is a good man.
He is so funny and fun, spending much time with me.
I like that, so he is the best dad anybody could ask for,
And I love him so much.
He sometimes makes me food like he did today,
And it was amazing.
He is so hardworking, and I love him so much
That I wrote this poem just for him
Because he is the best dad ever.

My dad is fun to be around.
He makes sure I study my books
And gives me a laptop
To complete my exploration of learning
For at least one hour every day.
My dad tells me I am the best daughter in the world
And that whatever I want to become, I can achieve it.
So, I have to study hard to take care of my mum and dad
When they grow old.

My dad always checks on me and my sister
When we are sleeping
So we don't sleep wrongly on the bed to avoid neck pain.
My dad is such a caring, loving person,
And he is always studying.
My dad ensures that there's always food in the house
And that we don't lack anything.
My mum is very supportive of my dad
And ensures that we respect everyone
And treat everyone alike,
Irrespective of where they come from.

My dad is my hero!
You hold my hands since I was born.
There is no better dad in the world than my daddy.
I will watch you as you guide me through this life,
For with you, I am safe from harm.

You are my hero, and words are not enough
To tell you how much you mean to me.
I will always look up to you, for you are my rock.
I will ensure that your expectations of me are met.
I will not let you down.
My dad, my hero!

I love you so much, Dad!

Annabelle Eromosele (8)

For Granted

I'm writing our last chapter
And I don't know how it ends
But the one thing I do know
Is that lovers don't end up friends
I tie my hair up with a pen tucked behind my head
Looking at our last message
I throw out the entire book across my bed
You know I'm good at writing
I could say exactly what I mean
But I just stare at it for months
What a romance novel seen.

I don't know where we go from here
You know I said it as a joke
"Where are they now?" not speaking
That was one of the last times we ever spoke
I look back at my notes
What exactly happened there?
I could end the story here
But would you think that that's unfair?

I close my eyes and imagine myself in your brain
Because what the hell are you thinking?
Driving me so incredibly insane
I wanna give it a happy ending
Because I want that for me

But I want someone you know on the first date
Not change their mind after three.

Someone who talks to my family
And then brings me home
Not someone that says, "I want to be together"
But then leaves me alone
I haven't been able to write a new character
Since you made our romance into a mystery
And my favourite subject was always science
But now I'm wasting time on our history.

I could rewrite the beginning
Remove some of my hope
Delete you altogether
That would be one way to cope
Make our romance into a tragedy
What would Romeo and Juliet say?

I was holding out for our future
But for you, it's just another day
At least it seems
Only one of us is a writer
So the other chooses to fight
So why do I stay the fighter?
I don't want to be a fighter

I don't want to be a part of some game
I want the 'after meeting you
Nobody could have ever made me feel the same'.

I don't want to create us
Put to words what we do
Why do I have to be the one to write
When someone tells me, "I love you."

There's magic in madness
All these things I've made
Why do I have to be courage
When somebody else gets to be afraid?

So what will it be then
These choices you make?
Because I am not someone
Who for granted you take.

Gracie Roberts (16)

In The Garden Of Words

In the garden of words, where the sun softly gleams,
There blooms my hero, whose name is but dreams.
No mother, no father, no brother, no kin,
But a poet whose verses reside deep within.

Emily Dickinson, in her room of seclusion,
Wove worlds from silence, a boundless illusion.
Her words were a fortress, her rhymes a pure light,
Guiding my soul through the darkest of night.

In quiet and solitude, she found her grace,
A recluse with a pen, setting hearts to race.
She spoke to the living, the dead and the skies,
With whispers of truth and enchanting sighs.

Her slant of the truth, like a prism of hue,
Unveils the unseen, the old and the new.
In metaphors wrapped, her wisdom lies still,
Inspiring my pen with a fervent will.

So here's to my hero, in shadows she stayed,
Yet her words are a sun that will never fade.
In the garden of words, her legacy grows,
A beacon of light where the wildflower blows.

Zafreen Chowdhury (15)

Whispers Of Time: A Journey Through Life

In the soft embrace of twilight's glow,
Memories whisper like the wind's gentle flow,
Of days long past, where laughter sang,
And family bonds in hearts firmly rang.

Childhood dreams, in fields we'd play,
Unbound by time, forever to stay,
The warmth of love, unrequited, yet pure,
In silent shadows, it did endure.

Amid the chorus of joy and delight,
Moments of happiness, pure and bright,
Yet, hand in hand with sorrow's kiss,
Sadness and loss, in life's abyss.

Fear and anxiety, shadows that creep,
Through sleepless nights, in silence they seep,
Yet hope and resilience, like morning's ray,
Dispel the darkness, herald a new day.

The call for justice, a voice so clear,
Equality's dream, ever near,
In hearts united, strength we find,
A world renewed, by love defined.

Traditions whisper from days of old,
Stories of heritage, courage bold,
In modern life, technology's gleam,
Yet human touch, a timeless dream.

What is life, but a fleeting dance?
Mortality's thread, in every glance,
Yet echoes of immortality's song,
In hearts and stars, forever long.

The universe, a vast embrace,
Human connection, cosmic grace,
In art's creation, we find our muse,
Inspiration's flame, the soul's true hues.

The artist's brush, a tender touch,
A dance with time, a story as such,
In every stroke, a world unfurled,
The beauty, power, and mystery of the world.

Through triumphs high and struggles deep,
In self-reflection, secrets keep,
The past a mirror, the future bright,
In introspection, find the light.

Nature's beauty, a timeless lore,
Mountains, forests, oceans' roar,
The power and mystery in every leaf,
A world of wonder, beyond belief.

In twilight's glow, as day meets night,
Memories dance in the fading light,
A tapestry woven, with threads of gold,
Life's story told; in hearts it's hold.

For in this journey, through joy and pain,
We find ourselves, again and again,
In every heartbeat, a tale unfurls,
A testament to this wondrous world.

Claire Olajide (14)

Miranda, My Hero

Miranda is so barmy,
her jokes wouldn't last in the army.
Now we're talking, aren't we? So let me begin my story
of Miranda and her glory.
Well, she fell in love with a guy
and is obsessed with food like pie.
She's full of funny jokes
but also a fan of lots of blokes.
She can be quite insane,
though her mother is a pain.
She has small friends made of fruit
and although they're from a root,
she still thinks they're rather cute.
She has a friend called Stevie, who can be lots of fun
but only when her work is done.
She makes up childish games
by calling people lots of names.
She's crazy, silly and lots of fun.
Prefers to gallop instead of run.
She lives in a flat on top of a shop
but now we're coming to a stop.
I'm sorry that we're done
but didn't we have such fun?
We're now at the end
and now you know about my friend.

Pegi Barnes (9)

The Battle Of Britain

It was a gloomy morning when,
All at once the alarms all sounded,
And all the aviators rushed to their Spitfires,
For the Luftwaffe were coming.
With a deafening roar they rose to the sky,
Looking for bombers to target and enflame.
Agile and nimble were their Spitfires,
Twisting and turning, looking for the Luftwaffe that were coming.

There a voice came over the radio, "They're above us!"
And so the squadron of twenty climbed up to fire hell on them,
Up they flew ready to fire hell on the Luftwaffe,
With all they had.
Their duty, their honour,
To defend the country they knew,
Shun their lives,
Shun their children and their wives,
Their duty to do and die.

Bomber to the right of them,
Bomber to the left of them,
Bomber in front of them,
Fired shot and shell,
But the warbirds dodged and weaved,
Valiantly cut through their lines,
Occasionally firing a few bursts,
That determined the lumbering bomber's fate.

Used all their guns bare,
Until their birds tumbled from the air,
Enflaming the beast here,
Enflaming the beast there,
Cutting the army to the shreds.
But then the enemy's backup came around,
Diving at them, their warbirds cutting through,
The brave aviators.
They recoiled from the warriors,
Dodging and weaving.
They flew back, but not,
Not the valiant twenty.

Enemy to the right of them,
Enemy to the left of them,
Enemy behind them,
Fired at by shot and shell,
Stormed at by the enemy,
While hero and warbird fell from the sky.

They who had fought so well,
Storming the enemy with shot and shell,
Came back from the sky of hell,
Protecting their homeland,
While hero and warbird fell from the sky.
When can their glory fade?
O the courageous battle they put up,
Defending us from certain death.
Honour the heroes!
Honour the protection they gave!
Honour them!

Harry Gu (9)

Is It True To Be You?

The field is green, there are lots of trees,
With lots of flowers and lots of bees.
But bit by bit,
Buildings are eating it.
Who can help me? My friends, my family,
Grandad, Granny, Mummy, Daddy.
My brother Logan, is that Great-Granny?
Friends Lilly, and Emma, Amelia and Abbey.
The dogs too can help - Jessie and Mavie,
And not forgetting another dog Maggy.
I said, "Help," they said, "No, you can do this on your own,
Believe in yourself, do it on your own."
Suddenly I was wearing a nice dress and good shoes,
And a crown on my head, then a voice said some news.
"Take all these gifts, I know you are strong.
Tell your family and friends to all do the same,
To make the world greener must be your aim."
I imagined a spell book with words I could say,
To make all the buildings go away.
Now the field is green with lots of trees,
Lots of flowers and lots of bees.

Immy Oliver (9)

My Past Life Self Is My Hero

Last night,
I went to sleep crying,
But,
Last night I also had a dream,
A dream so surreal yet something so real in it.
To know,
To experience we are more than what we see when we look in the mirror,
What happened before us?
Before this physical body and what happens after?
To know, now I know, after last night,
I'm more than what I've been seeing when brushing my teeth over the bathroom sink.
I saw the reflection of me every day, not thinking anything of it, thinking this is just me, this will always be me, always has been,
As of last night, I was proven wrong.
Last night I found out what happened before the creation of my reflection.
I saw a different reflection, one that I saw 24 hours before I was birthed in the now,
Before I was born in this time.

I saw an inspirational, gentle man with such similarities to me but wasn't the me now,
Not me in the present,
But me in the past? Yes.
I was shown life was worth carrying on with,
The tears I was shedding that night were soon to pass,
Soon to pass in time,
Soon, soon, whenever that was,
They would,
It was temporary.
Everything was temporary, I was experiencing on Earth,
But me, my soul, was forever.
I saw memories I made when I was this man, he explored, he cared, he inspired, he gave back, he had his fair share of tears, his ups and downs,
but he fought, he even fought through seas.
I was a sailor, who could handle the toughest waves there were.
This dream I had last night made me feel like I could do anything,
This man, who was I, was truly inspiring, you couldn't help but look up to him,
Now I know what I can do, I can feel the strength I once had, my past life's strength.
Never thought a dream would teach me so much, never thought I would meet a hero in a dream and that hero would be me.
Last night was something you would only imagine in fictional tales, doesn't mean tales cannot be real.

I can now feel and have now earned, been inspired, felt the strength, I once had coursing my veins.
My past life self is my hero.

Francesca Budnyj (18)

Football Legend

- **C** ompetitive and a focused footie player
- **R** obust, middle-aged man, born on the fifth of February 1985
- **I** mpressive striker full of hope and has achieved set goals in life
- **S** kilful and full of passion to play on the pitch
- **T** eam-orientated and energetic
- **I** nspiration to his fans nationally and internationally
- **A** drenaline-fuelled and fast-paced
- **N** ever gives up and is open-minded
- **O** utstanding performances with five Ballon d'Or trophies.

- **R** eliable and an ingenious team player
- **O** riginates from Portugal and is a family man
- **N** otable player known globally
- **A** mbitious and started his football career at the age of seventeen
- **L** egendary footballer and famous worldwide
- **D** etermined and a disciplined team player
- **O** ptimistic and possesses extraordinary football skills.

Lazzaro Pasquariello (13)

The Court Of A Youthful Legacy

She found herself fastened with her stride,
Her textbooks and racquets,
Became her new teenage weaponry to pursue her future,
Classrooms bright and courts so wide,
A balance struck,
Pushing a life well-voiced.

A levels pursued,
Textbooks shut,
Classrooms departed,
Fame distant,
Pursuit in reach.

But beneath the moon's dainty button,
A reflective sheen hung down,
Her dark, black abyss of hair,
Her coltish legs,
Her smiling, expressive eyes,
That embellishes nature,
Portraying her optimism - no one could erase,
The prospect of her zenith seemed unclouded,
As pure as gold.

Becoming the pretender to the court,
In vibrant white,
As her youthful heart contained fire,
Now untamed,
Each match a line,
Each win a page,
In stories where her spirit flamed.

Amidst the crowd's electric hum,
She danced on New York's ground,
Towards the cusp of womanhood,
The flaming ball of rage shot down bullets,
Scarring her young, pure eighteen-year-old alabaster skin,
Yet no signs of strain,
No hint of numbness,
In triumph's shout, her name resounded.

Emma Raducanu.

With every serve,
Every graceful swing,
Every volley,
And her every smash she leapt,
Game to a match to a set,
To a champion!

She won the Open,
Fragile and brutal,
Within courts where champions learnt to soar,
Her legacy remained,
A tale of striving, seeking more.

Her story, one of strength retold,
Silver spoons refused,
Easy lanes dismissed,
A path carved through grit and grind,
Throughout a focused plane,
A harmony of heart and mind.

Now my guide through life's relentless race,
In every swing, in who we are,
We see her strength.
Her endless grace,
Her determination,
Her resilience,
My hero.

Ayan Sinha (15)

The Chosen One

You encourage without knowing.
When the truth collapses on me.
You are there without showing.
When the truth is a beautiful yet terrible thing.
You will know that fame isn't everything.

Growing up you tried and tried.
Were born as the seventh month died.
Little did we know a great author would arise.
Being told that you're getting into your head.
But no one asked your opinion.

It's sort of exciting, isn't it?
Knowing you've helped people get through struggles.
Reading about a skinny little boy under the moonlit.
Stars wishing a life away from the Muggles.
You never gave up and neither will I.

When I'm older in many years to come.
Some will move on to things bright and young.
Ask what I read, turning the page with my thumb.
"After all this time?" they will say.
"Always."

Laura Orosz (14)

Tapestry Of Life

In this hallowed hall, I feel so out of place,
A misfit among peers with a different grace.
Their accents roll with ease, a melody so grand,
While my tongue stumbles, an outsider in this land.

Oh British high school, a world I can't embrace,
Where traditions bond and laughter finds its place.
I'm a stranger in this realm, an alien in disguise,
My heart aches for a home where I truly belong,
Where I can recognise.

Their uniform, a badge of pride they wear,
A symbol of unity, but I feel no share.
Their jokes and banter, I can't comprehend,
Like a foreign language that I'll never apprehend.

Oh British high school, a world I can't embrace,
Where traditions bond and laughter finds its place.
I'm a stranger in this realm, an alien in disguise,
My heart aches for a home where I truly belong,
Where I can recognise.

I yearn for a place where my spirit can soar,
Where I'm not judged by the clothes I wear or the words I adore.
A place where diversity is celebrated, not concealed,
Where I can be myself, my true colours revealed.

In this tapestry of life, I long to find my thread,
A place where I can weave my dreams, where my soul can be fed.
Until then, I'll wander these halls, an outsider's plight,
Yearning for a connection, a beacon in the night.

Oh British high school, a world I can't embrace,
Where traditions bond and laughter finds its place.
I'm a stranger in this realm, an alien in disguise,
My heart aches for a home where I truly belong,
Where I can recognise.

But I won't give up hope, I'll keep searching for my place,
Where I can fit in, where I find my grace.
For in the tapestry of life, there is a thread for every soul,
And I'll keep weaving until I find my perfect role.

Joy Green (12)

Till Her Lips Bled Red

Oh, Marilyn, oh sweet Marilyn Monroe
Even as your eyes are closed in death, they won't let you rest
You sold your life for gold, not physical, just visible cents paid for that dress
Even now, they're still using your mould
Was it worth it? The honest truth you thought you were told
Even so, I won't name and shame, I am one and the same
Truth long old to be told
I love your pain.

Your dress like gales I basked in
Marry a Jackie, not Marilyn
Made-up lips like thieves' mask
Out of my lips, I want not to be her
But you for I love that red from your lips
Even as they bled till blue, that showed the true Marilyn no one knew
All they cared for was your lips, not your head, you're all that they could reach to kiss
It would be a lie to say I do not think you are so pretty
That your vanity's bliss wasn't half the reason I want to be you, to bat eyes like yours so ditty.

Both halves sit in the lap of infatuation
The other ugly so makeup hid it with determination
Poverty-stricken, orphaned desperation
Rags to riches, Hollywood's prime, but yours seems different
Even through the struggle you did so with grace not one time did I think you crawled or differed in your pace
You worked your way up in the way I depict you to be and me to want to be with the heart not displaced.

That is why I want to live, breathe and give as you
No one have I seen has devotion as pretty as one's face
No one have I seen look so beautiful yet have a working heart so true
But as you said, we all grow old and cold in the end but your charm lives on, no cracks, it won't bend
What a tragedy that charm was to be the very thing that brought you to your bed, my lips read words and sweetly said
"Oh, Marilyn, oh sweet Marilyn Monroe."

Angel Jacobs (14)

My Hero: Sir David Frederick Attenborough

D iving into the world of nature, he explores the world all around
A ttention taken to every detail, every colour, every sound
V ariating explorations, pole to pole, rallying the forces of the sunset
I nsects, mammals, birds, fish and reptiles, he learns with an open mindset
D reaming many a book, winning no less than a rosette

F inding animals everywhere, exploring places never seen before
R iding the waves, all the way to the Caribbean shore
E xpecting many an interview, sharing his knowledge to people galore
D aring adventures such as those with colonies of feisty Adélie penguins, each one worthy to be globally headlined
E xtraordinary discoveries, that most could never find
R egarding every detail with great care, storing many facts in his highly capable mind
I chthyosaurs, sauropods, T-rex, history's not concealed
C reatures discovered, a new world revealed
K alinga prize, BAFTA, all in his field

A dventures in the Amazon, it never stops
T rekking the Himalayas, placing flags on mountaintops
T eaming up with animal specialists
E ntering the world of scientists
N ever downhearted, never afraid
B eaming bright smile to a vivacious parade
O rang-utans, giraffes, bears
R accoons, tasting many exotic pears
O pening a world with animals to rule, a land stowed away, deep in forgotten lairs
U nder low-hanging trees, wading through mounds of golden sand
G rand prizes, all delivered by regal hand
H urrah for Sir David Attenborough, because of him our knowledge of nature is so grand.

Rebecca Yang (8) & Michelle Do (8)

Bangtan Forever

B eyond what everyone thinks they are, BTS.
A ngels with no negative attitude, just burning flames of passion, kindness and love.
N othing can stop me from loving them, an unchallenged truth.
G reatest of all times, they inspire and teach that to forget everything and run isn't always the answer,
T ruly are jewels of happiness and fountains of euphoria, they taught us to love ourselves.
A rmies have a reason to why their ocean of self-love, awe and happiness has a chance of never running out.
N ever have I seen people like as them, so ethereal, so humble and over the top. They show we can be like that too.

S even shining souls like gold, their songs and music just rip the sadness out of you.
O nes who can never be replaced, everyone's light and hope, keeping me alive.
N ever giving up, kept working until they rose. Kept working hard until they reached their goal.
Y our Magic Shop resides forever in my heart, healing and comforting. They showed that everyone has their own galaxy.

- **E** ternally by our sides and true, and always themselves.
- **O** rdinary? No, they're more than that, and taught us to face everything and rise.
- **N** ever running away from the hardships they had to face, just for us.
- **D** uring the lowest times in my life they helped me up. There is no one else like them in the world, showing me that no darkness is eternal
- **A** lways have constellations of gratitude and love for them, though I know it's still not enough.
- **N** ever will the millions of glowing purple lights that love them fade away.

Akshara Madur (13)

Stephen Hawking

Stephen Hawking young and bright,
Was always focused on the cosmos at night.
Such an elegant, besuited gent,
He created theories and started his ascent.

Esteemed cosmologist
And scientist,
Stephen wrote a 'Brief History of Time'
It is a best-seller and is so sublime!

He saw life in a different way.
But then one day,
He was paralysed.
Constrained to a wheelchair he was terrorised.
What was going to happen to this brilliant mind?

He fought with much pride,
With Jane by his side.
Created the 'Theory of Everything',
What a clever thing.

It followed simple rules.
Some were even taught in school!
But then he realised,
It was not idealised.

He gave up on that.
But did not fall flat.
And then came the famous 'Hawking radiation'.
What a dense situation!

Died later than the doctors had said;
He is still talked about and read.
Kurt Godel's work was his friend,
But only to a certain extent!

He never gave up.
He wasn't even able to drink from a cup!
But always held strong.
Sometimes he could be wrong.
But he always came back along.

He created the world we live in today.
We can thank him for leading the way.
Who doesn't look up to him,
Whose life is extremely grim.

He can be glad,
That he didn't die mad.
And now he will sleep,
And never will he weep.

Look up at him as a father
And also as a brother.
He was more than just a man.
He is the fact that Everything began.

Lily Passeron (13)

A Champion Forever

The 22-year-old man joined Formula One in 2007,
He joined McLaren and became Alonso's teammate.
After losing the championship to Räikkönen by one point,
The destined dominator made up for that anguish,
And won the 2008 championship against Massa by one point.
He took a new route in his long journey,
By joining Mercedes at twenty-eight years old.
He won his second World Championship in 2014,
And became a three-time champion in 2015.
By losing the 2016 title to Rosberg by five points,
He unleashed his dominant form,
And earned the next four World Champion titles in a row.
He broke Schumacher's record of the most wins in F1 history,
And aimed to be an eight-time World Champion,
But in 2021, Verstappen beat him by eight points.
Now, he still drives known as a seven-time World Champion,
And he will always be known as a seven-time World Champion.
This is Lewis Hamilton, a champion forever.

Pone-Pone Htet (11)

Nanny, Mummy And The NHS

Thank you to all the NHS workers, you all do an amazing job

"Emergency ambulance, is the patient breathing?"
"Help, help! Nanny's in a pickle,
She has a dodgy ticker
And her breathing's in a wiggle."

"Tell me your location
And we can see what we can do!
I am sending you an ambulance
And a paramedic too."

Nee-naw, nee-naw!
The flashing lights are here
To pick up Nanny
As they bring in all their gear.

They rush her to the hospital
As they wish the roads to clear.
I'm scared, I'm worried, I'm in a panic,
And now I shed a tear.

They wheel the bed into the ward,
The consultants gather around,
Along with the doctors and the nurses
To see what can be found.

The pharmacist preps the meds
While the bed is being made.
The nurse is looking after her
As the pain begins to fade.

The doctor comes by the next day
And says Nanny can go home.
But if her symptoms worsen
She needs to phone 111.

A cardiology referral
Is what Nanny needs
To make sure the heart
Doesn't get any disease.

Two million loyal workers
Who scrub and cook and clean
To make sure we're all healthy,
Fit for our king and queen.

They change the beds and heal the wounds
And sew the gashes back together,
Drive patients home, answer the phones,
We need them here forever.

To all the staff who helped my nanny,
Who are true experts in their fields,
Nanny's feeling better now
And her heart is nearly healed.

Charlie Kirk (9)

Mr McGowan

He arrives at early dawn in his teaching empire
Children upon children like a choir
Working away the little ones must
The wise one at his desk creating knowledge to trust.

Pulling up information on a board like a wizard
Words and symbols fly at you like a blizzard
His smarts cannot be unmatched, he is most clever
One of the best teachers, his students say, ever.

Then, at the football pitch, his skills peerless
Kicking the ball, amazingly fearless
Manchester United is his idol team
Man City, his rival, he hates, and that, he does mean.

He plays guitar like a soothing tune
It leaves the children dancing till moon
Bob Marley his man
Mmbop is his jam.

I don't know what else to rhyme
So I give some precious time
I will stop this poem while it's fine
And play some games of mine.

James Davenport (10)

My Heroes

I don't just have one hero,
There are many who inspire me,
People from all around,
Read on to find out and see...

Singing is my passion,
I like Ed Sheeran the best,
I like to practise all his songs,
He's better than the rest.

Ed Sheeran brings out lots of songs,
'Bad Habits' is my favourite one,
I like to sing it all the time,
It's lots and lots of fun!

Another person who is my hero,
Is Olivia, my best friend,
We may fall out sometimes,
But our friendship will never end.

We sometimes sit together for lunch,
And then she might play with me,
She comes over to my house,
And then she stays for tea.

Someone else who I am close to,
Is Emilie C, who's always there,
I know to get a friend like her,
Is very, very rare!

Emilie always listens to me,
When I need to talk something through,
She lets me play her games,
And she is very kind too!

My mum, because she takes care of me,
I know I can always talk to her,
She helps me if I need it,
And that's what I prefer.

She plays Barbies a lot with me,
And together we read a book,
We play tennis at the park,
And she helps me if I'm stuck.

My dad is also my hero,
He is really, really funny,
He loves to play water bombs,
And puts the hot tub up when it's sunny.

He's also on with my bedroom,
I think he is really great,
He's really good at fixing things,
And he's a really good mate!

These are all my heroes,
Who I am very grateful for,
They are all a big part of me,
I couldn't love them any more!

Ella Nicholls (8)

Luminous Presence

Within the bustling halls of school,
Where laughter rings and whispers rule,
One figure stands with radiant grace,
Their presence, a warm and guiding embrace.

Their laughter, a melody that fills the air,
Dispelling worries, banishing despair.
With every smile, they light the way,
In the ebb and flow of each school day.

In moments of struggle, they shine bright,
Their strength and courage, a guiding light.
When shadows linger, and doubts arise,
They're the one who clears the skies.

In a sea of faces, they shine so true,
My guiding light in all I pursue.
In every lesson, they play a part,
For in my school, they hold my heart.

So here's to you, my guiding star,
In you, I find who you truly are.
Through every class, until the end,
My favourite person, my cherished friend.

Aisha Desai

My Family, My Heroes

In a world full of chaos and noise
There is one constant that brings me joy
My family, my heroes, my kin
They stand by me through thick and thin
Through all of life's ups and downs
They are the ones who wear the crown.

My mom, with her gentle touch
Her words of wisdom, I cherish so much
She is the glue that holds us together
Through stormy weather, she remains steadfast
Always putting others before herself
A true embodiment of love and grace.

My dad, the pillar of strength
His unwavering support knows no length
He works tirelessly to provide for us all
His sacrifice and dedication, never small
A foundation of integrity and honour
A role model for me to look up to.

My brother, my partner in crime
With him, life is never dull or a mime
We share so many laughs and inside jokes
A bond that cannot be broken by any strokes
He is always there to have my back
In him, I've found a forever friend, no lack.

My sister, my playful cheerleader
Her antic jokes make me a succeeder
Angelic face full of laughter
Full of energy, she is hard to look after
A bond between us that nothing can sever
In her, I've found a lifelong companion forever.

Together, we are a unit strong
A family bond that will never go wrong
Through trials and tribulations, we stand tall
Together, we rise above and achieve all

My family, my heroes, my everything
With them by my side, I can conquer anything.

Hafsa Muhammad Nusair (13)

The Gentle Guide

In a world of wonders, there stands my uncle,
A beacon of kindness, his presence a miracle.
With glasses perched upon his nose so neat,
His wise, gentle eyes, a comforting retreat.

Five foot four, he may be small in height,
But his spirit soars, reaching great heights.
A grey beard adorns his face with grace,
A testament to the wisdom etched on his face.

His black hair, like a raven's wing,
Frames a soul that's pure, a heart that sings.
His tan skin, kissed by the sun's warm embrace,
Radiates warmth, kindness in every trace.

He listens with care, his ears attuned,
A friend in need, never leaving me marooned.
Through life's storms, he's my steady guide,
His wisdom and presence forever by my side.

His kindness, a river that endlessly flows
Like a gentle breeze, his compassion shows.
With every word, a seed of hope he sows,
His love and support, a treasure that grows.

His wisdom, a lighthouse in the night,
Guiding me through darkness with its light.
He shares his knowledge, a beacon so bright,
Nurturing my dreams, igniting them with might.

His helpfulness, a gift beyond measure,
Lending a hand, bringing joy and happiness.
He works tirelessly to keep my heart light,
A smile on my face, even on the darkest night.

My dear uncle, so special, so true,
With a heart of gold that shines through.
In his presence, happiness finds its place,
A bond unbreakable, filled with love and grace.

Marcela Demcak (13)

A Traveller's Farewell

You left us and we suddenly lost all sense of reality
Has it taken us over - insanity?
Is it that maybe you have travelled and are coming back?
Such irony!
You're a traveller and are never coming back.

I wished the strong one with whom you have companionship was right
That you left like Moses and like Moses you would return...
How wrong he was in his state of anguish, sobbing fiercely as his legs gave way
When you came, my beloved, the whole city was filled with such joy it reached the very corners and in-between,
The *noor* felt like it would never seep back down into the soil and desert sand below
But you left us with a sweet smile
Hoping for the companionship of the most Noble, most High.

You travelled for many long years in such you witnessed wonders and calamities
There was an angelic feeling when amazing words befell you
Eyes spectated the message you carried
Hearts proclaimed it fully with joy!
Would you invite me, my beloved?
So that I can kiss your hand and vocalise my salam?

Though you have never seen me
And I have never seen you.

But you are gone from the world people run towards - smiling
And you embraced the true reality of death that strikes horror into the hearts of men
Lend me your company, O my beloved
So that my heart may cry
To the very one who you ran to.

Will you intercede for me on a magnificent day where random shan't be accepted?
On a terrible day on which we shall meet?

Rashida Khan (15)

The Rare Gem

Who is your hero?
I gaze, amazed at my idol,
Compassionately giving a fresh apple to a ragged, poor homeless person,
Whose face was covered in grimy ashes, she shivered like she was in the snow.
Smiling like the sun, the hero radiated warmth and at once, the woman ceased to shiver
The hero did not expect niceness back, but the woman thanked her warmly.
For every day, people laughed cruelly at her poor condition and treated her badly as if she was below them.

Who is your hero?
My hero drew out her money with motivation to share,
Driven by the sight of the hungry, ill children sleeping on the dusty pavement,
And offered it to the exhausted, tired, kind charity worker.
The worker was dumbfounded by the huge, colossal amount of money,
She was tearful, joyful and grateful and accepted it graciously.
My hero smiled at the sight of the happy, thin woman with dark circles under her eyes crying out joyfully.
She did not see a difference between others and her.

Who is your hero?
My hero has a bright, shiny smile,
That warms the hearts of many people.
I adore my hero and admire her,
For she perfectly protects others from harm with the belief that it's her duty.
I love my hero because she is funny,
Smart, kind, cheerful and honest, she is the light of the world.
My hero believes even if others have stopped doing good, you can continue, nevertheless.

Debbie Wong (9)

One And Only Enhypen

O ne and only shining brightly like in the pitch black a guiding star,
N avigating through obstacles and overcoming failure no matter how dark.
E verything with passion, hard work and originality in each stride,

A nd always fuelling each performance with determination and pride.
N o one can ever take away their talent or their true celestial place,
D reamers of ambition, aiming like fate's arrows, success they embrace.

O f course they can keep eternally rising, reaching their true potential,
N ever giving up, finding the joy in this journey, they'll always be influential.
L evelled high, these unique idols are humble yet stand tall and strong,
Y es, they are and forever will be one and only, in our hearts where they belong.

E ach member a star with their dazzling light, Enhypen shine bright,
N ever before or now failing to dominate the stage with their might.
H olding their heads and spreading their wings like the angels they are,
Y et being that everlasting tower of beauty and magic for us Engenes afar.
P erfection radiates from them, between us and them a bond tightly spun,
E clipsing all doubts, no matter what, wherever they're at, they've won.
N ow ready or not, here they come.

Adithi Madur (13)

Self-Acclaiming The Throne - My Favourite Person: Yours Truly

I'm my favourite person, and I'm proud to say,
I'm a masterpiece, in every single way.
I ace my exams, with a smile so bright,
And talk with grown-ups, with wisdom and insight.

My hazel eyes sparkle, like diamonds in the night,
My brown skin glows, with a radiant light.
I'm literally perfect, don't you agree?
I'm a work of art, in every single way.

I dance like a dream, with steps so fine,
In Western and Indian styles, I'm truly divine.
I'm a future film director, with a vision so grand,
And my writing skills are simply out of hand.

I'm a lyricist, with words that flow like gold,
My songwriting skills are worth more than all the gold.
I'm the master of my area, don't you forget,
I'm the best version of myself, and I won't regret.

So stop being green-eyed, it's not worth the pain,
Just accept that I'm awesome, and I won't change.
I'll keep on shining, like a star in the night,
And you can just sit back, and enjoy the show with delight.

I'm my favourite person, and I'm proud to say,
I'm the best version of myself, every single day.
And forever and forever, I'm my own superhero,
You can watch me go places, and be in zero.

Shruthi Dushyanthan (12)

Here You Were

Here you were so long ago,
Your hair burnt brighter than this sorrowful sun...

But then a harrowing, hollow wind hushed you along,
And left only a charred star where your glory used to stand.

Your weird power, whatever it may be,
Slashed a healing mark into my heart:
Not the mark of oppressive yells and shouts in a distant isolation,
But one so foreign, like a cheap paper golden star.

So I shall keep parading it around to my friends;
I shall keep telling your story through empowered sobs:
"She never gave up on me.
She only saw light in my eyes streaming with bullets
Carefully loaded by those tyrants.
She took those empty shells and shot them far into the sky,
And they erupted with colours so mystical,
That I felt a surreal pride, a glowing joy
Come fantastically alive within me.
For a second, I almost thought
I was someone else entirely,
Because how could I:
Useless, voiceless, mindless,
Have this beauty ablaze inside me?"

Even horses look at their leather-lined blinkers,
Glued together by their forefathers,
And they feel, like a powerful gust,
The sigh of victory into history.

Here you will always be:
Your memory will never be snuffed out by life's misery.

Bobby Grigore (16)

We Can Be Heroes

Everyone is a hero,
Even if they don't think so.
Heroes like doctors, the police and firefighters,
Make our day so much brighter.

Don't forget sharing is caring;
Donate things to the poor including your sparing.
Try to be friends with everyone you know,
So our friendship rate can grow, grow, grow.
Help each other all of the time,
Because helping is equally prime.

You can be a hero any day you want;
Being a hero means encouraging people,
Especially if they're gaunt.
Being a hero means helping no matter what,
Being a hero means using the talents you've got.

Heroism isn't just for strong people,
Everyone can do it, even the feeble.
Right or wrong is normally a choice you have to make,
Or maybe saying something true or something fake.

It doesn't matter if you're rich or poor,
So do whatever you can to just soar.
Many people believe in you, even me,
There are so many different ways to be heroes,
Just wait and see.

Maybe saving the environment, or recycling correctly,
Can save nature and the planet,
So everyone will be merry.
Stop children from being bullies,
So the world can be populated,
With not baddies but goodies.

Dhruti Shreekumar (10)

Obscurer

A fresh knock on the door sent my hand to press
The handle softly down and let it return to rest.
The guest hovered past our console table, searching
For a seat.
Mum as usual,
Like Indiana Jones, led them to where they were meant to be.

Before keeping up, her eyes spotted a familiar sight,
Our small frame on the table - had fallen forward
My memory fumbled to find when, but
Her fingers lifted it to face the sky.

In hopes of scratching off the glass slits,
Mistaking it for lint or stains,
Not one of them budged, slid or detached
But wrung out her endeavour of nail-gliding disdain.

The calling of my name pulled me away to a palm
Of the guest who waited patiently
To bridge a reciprocation of their charm.

After they left their crumb-freckled dish,
Mum asked about my new face of dejection,
As she struggled to balance the porcelain with some that sat beneath.

Muted is the courage that left my mouth,
To accept what no longer stood.

So today, she slots a new picture into the frame,
Still, the glass keeps showing cracks,
But the broken visual will be beautiful enough
To make the rest obscured.

Malaika Khan (15)

Mother, My Guiding Star

In the darkness of my life, you lead me with the brightest lamp
A beacon of love and joy that guides me through the gloom
Your hands are so special, they have built my world with care.

Your voice, a soothing melody in my heart
Has calmed my fears and filled my life with light
Through every horrible storm in my life, you are there for evermore to guide me again
In your warm embraces, my heart is always filled with happiness.

You are the gentle breeze when the day is gone
In your eyes, I always find the love
The love that you gave me ever since I was born
It's a love that fights and trials can not erase.

With every smile, you chase those lurking shadows away
Turning boring moments into a brighter day
Mother, you are my endless sea.

Boundless, nurturing, wild and free
In your love, I have found my treasured place
A heaven of warmth and an endless embrace.

So this is for you, my guiding star
You will always be forever cherished and forever dear
For your heart always has a place for me there
Forever loved, forever cared for
My mother, my guidance and my endless sphere.

Amaarah Hussain (12)

My Mom

My ultimate inspiration comes from a dazzling woman whom I call Mom,
She encourages me to do whatever I want to do,
Be whoever I want to be,
To not be afraid of who I am,
She taught me that my authenticity is my superpower,
She fills my home with fun and baking and books and laughter,
Filling my heart with love,
My head with positivity,
And my soul with the blessing of faith,
Introducing me to empowering figures,
Emmeline Pankhurst to Princess Diana,
Encouraging me to inherit the habits of fictional characters in the stories I'd be enlightened to,
Matilda to Hermione Granger,
She replenishes my life with an overwhelming drive to achieve and do her best,
While spending fifteen years sculpting and forming people to look up to,
Role models to follow,
Morals to obey,
To be kind, compassionate, brave, bold and one-of-a-kind,
To read and learn,
To paint and pick flowers,

To read classical literature and experience nature,
To smile and become the best version of myself,
In the midst of all this,
She never really knew,
The person who inspired me most was her!

Eleanor Price (15)

Change Of Thought

Who was the hero of my life?
When I once hid in the shadows
Afraid of coming out
When I lived with fear and hate
When no one bothered to help me fight.

I learnt to help myself
Distrust anyone who came near
I embraced every scar
Denied every tear.

Never forgot where I came from
The shambles that made me me
Like a phoenix from the ashes
I shed my skin and soared.

I now know who was the hero of my life
In those cold, miserable days
It was the hardships that shaped me
The hurt, hunger and strife
Of my young childhood days.

It may have hurt me
May have hurt that I was alone,
May have hurt that the world I lived in
Was a twisted broken mess.

But we learn to grow from what we go through
The troubles, the tests
We learn that a hero may not be
Someone with a cape.

The world was not made without
Horror and pain
But we were made to change that
To stand up again and again.

So if you ask me who the hero of my life was
I'll tell you that it had all along been life.

Amirah Shafii (12)

Marcus Rashford

In Manchester's streets where dreams ignite,
A young soul rises, shining bright.
Marcus Rashford, name of grace,
A beacon of hope, a smiling face.

With every kick, with every goal,
He plays with heart, he plays with soul.
On fields of green, under skies so wide,
He dances with purpose, with passion as his guide.

But more than sport, he chose to fight,
For children's hunger, for their rights.
With pen and voice, with love profound,
He lifts the lost, the voiceless found.

From humble start to hero's throne,
His journey shows what hearts have known.
That courage, kindness, spirit strong,
Can right the world of many wrongs.

Through trials faced and battles won,
He stands as proof of what can come,
When one believes, when one takes a stand,
To lend the world a helping hand.

So, here's to Marcus, beacon bright,
Your deeds inspire, your story lights.
For in your path, we see the way,
To build a better world today.

Zineddine Chennoufi (12)

Cristiano Ronaldo

In the realm of soccer's artistry,
One name shines with audacity,
Cristiano Ronaldo,
A maestro of the game.

The skills took hearts,
With dribbling,
And the shooting.

Ronaldo! Ronaldo!
Chanting the fans,
His name.

The destroyer of clubs,
Came from Madeira,
Wonderkid of football,
Has conquered Europe.
Won five Ballon d'Ors,
Won four Champions Leagues,
For Real Madrid,
Won one Champions League,
For Manchester United.

Now plays for Al Nassr,
And Portugal!

A true champion in all his glory,
On the pitch, he soars and he shines,
A footballer, the best in the land!

Started his career in sporting,
Went to Man United,
Real Madrid, Juventus,
Then came to Man United,
Now he is at Al Nassr.

His talent and dedication,
A sight to behold,
A master of the game,
His story untold.

Cristiano Ronaldo,
The true greatest of all time,
In football history.

Aydin Nasif (10)

Unbreakable Bond

His eyes are deep and dark
As deep as the ravine in the sea
As dark as the bottomless pit found in the deep
Your smile full of hope, that you find each day
How I wish to imitate that same smile
That brings brightness in every way
It guides me in the darkest nights
Some the darkest of days
Sometimes you catch me at the wrong time
When my anger has been set ablaze
I might seem mean and a snob
But I don't mean it that way
You leave me alone and I reflect
On what I have done, starting to say
"Oh, how your laughter fills the room
Your jokes always funny and unique"
Some days when I don't have anyone to talk to
You're the one who brings yourself to speak
Your voice a melody in my ear
Something I find fantastique
Our days might have their ups and downs
We're all made this way
And hey, all I wanted to say

I will always love you forever
My dear little, sometimes annoying
But wondrous brother.

Danielle Teknikio (13)

Suzanne Collins

An author she is
As her mind is a whizz
'The Hunger Games' she wrote
As she is afloat
Her heart is pure
As she is like a cure.

Famous, famous
Oh wow, oh wow
Remember her name
As she has a mane
Her book shows us truth
As in this game you may lose a tooth.

Her name starts with an 'S'
And ends in an 'e'
Love story quite not
As she needs to think of what.

Katniss is her model
As her life is trapped in a bubble
Courageous, kind
As survival is in her mind
Katniss is her girl
As life is a hurl.

Katniss' aim is striking
As she goes kiting
All I can see is a plan
Oh please fall in love.

She is free
As she passes a bee
Oh Hunger Games, oh Hunger Games
My mind is racing
As my heart is pacing
Is Katniss going to survive?
As a tree in her honour will thrive.

Please, please survive
As she can only think of home
Home, home once again
She survived, oh home
Just put on your gloves
As it's been a while
All you've got to do is smile...

Emelia Craddock (12)

For You

In quiet moments, when shadows fall,
I hear a voice, a clarion call.
A beacon bright in the darkest night,
Your spirit shines, a guiding light.

With strength, you face each daunting day,
No fear can turn your heart away.
You rise above the storm's embrace,
Determination in your grace.

Your words are sparks that light the flame,
Encouragement is your steady aim.
In every challenge, there you stand,
A rock, a shelter, a helping hand.

Your kindness, boundless, like the sea,
Inspires the best in those like me.
A heart so pure, with love to give,
You show us all just how to live.

In times of doubt, when courage wanes,
Your presence washes out the stains.
A pillar firm, unyielding, true,
The world is brighter thanks to you.

So here's my ode, my humble praise,
To you, who lights my darkest days.
For in your strength and boundless care,
I find my hope, my path, my air

Noor-Ul-Huda Mughal (12)

The Real Hero

A hero has no fear I read
Diamonds trickled reluctantly down Dad's cheeks
You are a hero, he said.

For when the dilemma is solved
The dark is lightened by a sun ray
When life gets old
The real hero does not save the day
They go their own way.

So a hero has fear
Yet they still push on
No matter what they see or hear.

Through the challenges of life
The highs and the lows
When words sink like a knife
No matter what, forwards they still go.

Do we know a real hero? I pondered
Curiosity building inside me
And into Dad's arms, I wandered.

There are people who do things for the best
We all have them inside us but
Some choose to let them rest
Some do what is right

No matter how many doors are shut
You are a real hero
I know from your kind words
For you, nothing is zero
You don't need to fly like a bird
The real hero is inside you.

Veya Berg (10)

Super Mum

Her beauty will blind you
And happiness will come,
When she fills you with joy
You will know she is my fabulous mum.

With a heart of gold
And with a mind so spontaneous,
For her anything is possible
And her love is contagious.

Spreading her love
Through every street,
Her voice leaves a song
That is so very sweet.

She changes the bad times
With every appearance she makes,
As she looks down on her children
She tells them they are her sponge cakes.

When guests come around
She starts to clean,
So when they begin to inspect
There is not a speck of dust to be seen.

But even then
The dust comes again,
Therefore she cleans even more
So the place is shinier than a diamond chain.

She will be my hero forever,
She never lets me down,
Through sun and rain
She always wears her *super dressing gown!*

Beata Kalthi (11)

My Hero

I don't know what I'd do without you
You are my inspiration
My role model
My one-of-a-kind mum
My hero.

No one can make me happy like you do
You are my happiness
My loved one
My irreplaceable mum
My hero.

No one in this world can ever replace you
You are my best friend
My greatest teacher
My partner in crime
My hero.

I wish you could see yourself the way I do
You are my world
My everything
My special mum
My hero.

I love the way you laugh
And how your smile lights up my day
Even when we get angry at each other
I love you like no other
You always try to encourage me
Even if I think I can't do it anyway
You're a kind-hearted and loving mother
You're the light to guide me when times are tough
Even this poem is not enough
To tell you how much I love you
My hero.

Eva Raghavendra (10)

The Mountain I Followed

We are family
One, to two, to three
We are like lock and key
Climbing the same mountain I did but along a different path
Yet our love is higher than that mountain's wrath.

We are family
I guide you along the right and wrong
Dreading the routes I took, long
Wishing my footsteps not to be repeated
As you trek, onward through the finite path of undiscovered mysteries depleted.

We are family
My love is an unedifying strife
Longer than life
You are my closest comfort, kindest crier
Tease, and snitch, I despair but understand love's desire.

We are family
The silver lining of love beams bright
Highlighting love's true fight
Side by side
Following the tide.

You are my brother
I love you so much
You are never alone
You are never unbound
I will help lead you into the light.

Frida Rocha (16)

Cleopatra

I will not be triumphed over,
By family, friend or foe,
For I am Cleopatra,
Your favourite female pharaoh,
I am always willing to learn,
The respect of people I can earn,
Many languages I can speak,
Ancient Egyptian and even Greek,
I dress like the goddess Isis,
I stand out in the street,
Stylish, clever, and cunning,
I am someone you want to meet,
I will not back down,
So don't mess with me,
I am ruthless and brave,
Ask Ptolemy and Ptolemy,
Men will not decide my future or indeed my fate,
You don't want to be my enemy,
It's better to be my mate!
When my husband was murdered in Rome,
I was left all alone,
Resilient as ever, I came back fast,
Not to be beaten by my sad past,

People will look up to me, even when I'm gone,
Girls can rule the world,
We are clever, brave, and strong.

Maya Beane (7)

Life On The Shelf

You are my life on the shelf,
Forever present, yet different to oneself,
Your heart of emotion, a blanket of mist,
My spark who's nought flickered away, he vanished.

Yet those who surround me,
And those who need ministering,
Shall never reach comfort,
From the heavy hugging of nature,
That my arms constantly grasp for history.

That very phone call,
Slicing my heart,
Tsunami of reality,
Was my flower who needed wilting,
My dad lay still,
Tasting his lost peace,
Took his life,
And was found there deceased.

No longer can parent me,
That I will not care,
As long as I have my life on the shelf,
I will never tear.

For, now you are my pot on the shelf,
Swarmed in dust, all by yourself,
Eternally spirit, and ever so far,
Yet still my dad, my heart, my life, my star.

Bayley Layton (13)

How You Helped Me

As you have brought up
An amazing child
Helped through struggles
In desperate need and hope
You were there.

When I was broken down
You caught me when I was falling
Or up and running
You always watched from the side
Even as you struggled and nearly passed to the next life
You always thought of us.

The crystal shards rolled down my face
But you moved them
Knowing they may pierce you
Not by touch but by heart.

As the memories flashback
Bullets shoot through me
Leaving me unable to breathe.

Wait a minute
Only now I realise
I wasn't the only one suffering but you too
You suffered more
So why couldn't I see it
Was I that blind?

Thank you
For the sacrifices
Challenges
Motivation
Words
Opportunities that you risked for yourself.

Haneefah Ali (12)

Focalistic, The Upbeat, Successful Hip Hop Artist!

Thank you for being a South African rapper!
I realised how you want to make music in your town called Pretoria.
Everyone has been enjoying it so far
And thinking you have been sensational!
And how you are a journalist in music,
You cover the world of music for print publications,
Online journals, magazines and broadcast media outlets
Like your father did when he passed away.

Focalistic, you should be proud of what you have achieved since 2016!
You have achieved a huge milestone into becoming a successful hip hop artist and a president!
You have come a long way.

Everyone in Pretoria's so proud to have you!
It means everyone a lot!
Wishing you all the best!
Many years to celebrate!
Keep being Pretoria's president and rapper!
Also, keep promoting your genre of music called Amapiano to the world!

Benjamin Doeteh (17)

Family Is Our Life

Even if we go our separate ways we will always love each other and care for each other because family is our life.
Why is our bond stronger than ever?
Why is my family, my cheerleaders?
Family is our life.
Family is beautiful, like a tree dancing in the wind,
We support each other like it is nothing.
We love each other with respect and honesty,
Family is our life. Why are we always there for each other like that?
Family is our life, we carry them everywhere we go, in our hearts.
Having my family in my life is like a lion protecting its cubs from the wild.
My family is my shield.
Family is different in every way.
Oh! What a beautiful family I have.
A family so beautiful!
Family is the sun in the sky big and bright.
Family is family - so bright and so awesome.
Family is our life.

Aisha-Eniola Tandjigora (9)

Chimamanda Ngozi Adichie

- **C** is for the creativity she shows, through her poems and novels.
- **H** is for her hope for the future authors and poets to come.
- **I** is for the intelligence of writing and the inspiration she gives to young writers and poets.
- **M** is for the marvellous books she has written.
- **A** is for her ambition to write inspirational books that change lives.
- **M** is for her motivation to help us become extraordinary like her.
- **A** is for her being articulate, having the ability to show her diverse heritage.
- **N** is for her country Nigeria where she is from, and how proud she is to say it. (I am Nigerian as well).
- **D** is for her desire to write, having an impact on Nigerian writers and writers worldwide.
- **A** is for her being assertive, being confident and positive all the time.

Chikaima Onyenyionwu (10)

My Grandad

My grandfather had a heart of gold
His story until now was never told.
He was the brains, he loved meals galore.
He loved his family and friends, always had room for more.
He had an open house.

He helped lots of people in need, his wisdom was close to none.

He helped my grandmother do housework,
He told me the story about the turtle and the hare
While I learnt to brush my hair.

He hunted like a pro, he was my pro!
And helped make my skin glow, his compliments filled with love.

The sun made him feel like he was melting
Yet the only melting was love in my heart.

His empathy remains unmatched.
Because he was extremely heavenly.

Even his demise will never take that from me.
For the love and care he shared,
I am extremely grateful.

Attalia Schultz-Nazim (10)

Siostry

I tread through the lingering corridor,
Bordered with barbed bushes,
They pierce my skin with each step,
Burgundy strokes and drops scatter on my skin.

It hurts, yet I see a yellow light at the end,
My skin prickles with blemishes of suffering.
The streams leak down my arms and legs,
Yet I am still alive.

No blood leaks from my heart,
My eyes and lips are unharmed,
The branches and thorns are held away.
Pairs of hands bend them away.

Scarred streaks line their porcelain skin,
Like the stripes of a tiger. A fighter. A guardian.
Such familiar hands, made with flesh and bone.
They gently shield and lead the way.

They allow my heart to love.
My lips to speak.
My eyes to see.
But they still let me experience life as it was meant to be.

Zuzanna Kalek (15)

Hope

My hero is the light that guides you through the darkest times,
Darkest hours,
Darkest crimes.
It's the light you see, at the end of the hall,
That guides you when nobody else wants to at all.
It's the light that brings your room to a fill,
And sees the good in you when nobody else will.
My hero is the one who believes in you,
Your pureness,
Your achievements.
It discovers the small spark you are,
And the small spark you have.
Even when that light gets shattered,
It builds you up until you're not fractured.
My hero is the light that you seek,
That we all value and treasure.
This small ink of hope belongs to me,
As I thankfully continue to live happily.
It's the hero I hold in my heart,
As I patiently wait for my journey to start.

Vera Krauchuk-Muzhiv (12)

Can We Really Be Heroes?

Can we really be heroes,
When we are so afraid
Of what others think?
Even when we have a parade?

Can we really be heroes,
Bathed in justice and glory,
When we are always the villain
In someone else's story?

Can we really be heroes,
When we won't let go
Of the guilt and shame
That continues to grow?

Can we really be heroes?
I can't possibly be.
For I am not worthy
Of being bestowed with glee.

Heroes make mistakes,
But I have made too many.
Are there things I regret?
Oh, there are plenty.

I'm a villain.
I have guilt.
I'm afraid
One day, I will wilt.

Now I have explained
How I am a walking zero.
Now answer my final question...
Can I really be a hero?

Ishpel Williams (14)

Usain Bolt

The lightning Bolt was one of the poorest,
But with sweat, he became the richest.
Some think he was fast from the start,
But he was not, his coach found his destiny.

His passion was so great that it made him,
Make a record that was not broken till now.
Day and night he trained and trained,
Behind every fame, there's always pain.

His love for the race was so great,
That the race loved him back.
There were times when he thought he couldn't race again,
But his desire took him to London.

I want to run towards my passion,
Just like Bolt.
No matter what obstacles I face,
I will keep on running.

No matter how hard the challenge is,
I will stand up and face it.
No matter what I face,
I will go past and then beyond.

Pranav Shake (11)

Our Super Cool Teacher

When Mr Redford comes to school,
His shoes are always shiny and cool.
He walks in with a smile on his face,
Every part of learning he will embrace.

When he's teaching, he's amazing and fun,
He goes the extra mile,
And is our number one.
Every class he shows good deeds,
And helps us grow from a little seed.

Barn Owls class is full of luck,
Mr Redford steps in when we're stuck.
No child is shy to ask a question,
The atmosphere is free of tension.

He makes us feel so welcome each day,
The classroom rules need to be obeyed.
In Year Six we'll always remember,
When we all joined his class in the month of September.

Goodbye and thank you once again,
You're the coolest teacher.
Who became our friend.

Arabella Pasquariello (10)

Taylor Swift

"You're on your own, kid," they would say
I'm not trying to exaggerate,
But a piece of me died right there
The happy in me faded away

I would go straight to my bed,
Play her music as soon as I got there
"No one wanted to play with me as a little kid," she sang
The only thing I felt like I could relate to was her.

What if I told you,
Being drawn to her music wasn't accidental,
She's a mastermind,
When everything has changed
And you've been left behind,
Forever and always,
She'll always be there
Shining like a mirror ball
To save me if I jump then fall

Taylor Swift saved me
When I was alone
When I felt like my life was ending
Straight away, I would play her songs on my phone.

Bella Hayes (13)

To My Best Friend

Since the start of the year, we have stood side by side
Each step we take, in each other we confide
From the memories we hold
Our friendship starts to unfold
I cannot imagine myself without you
It's like we are glue.
No matter what the weather
The tide will bring us together
Our friendship is perfect
It's just what I expect
A friend like you is a diamond in the rough
A friend like you is enough
You stand out within our peers
You are the only one that appears
This friendship is too good to be true
But we will stick together all the way through
Thank you for sticking with me all the way through
You're what a friend should be
You bring the quirkiness out of me.

I think I've just found a friend for life...

Imaan Rahman (12)

Mum, What Is A Superhero?

"Mum, what's a hero?" I would ask.
Her reply was,
"Some heroes can help others finish a task."
"Mum, you're my hero,
You are caring, loving and a lot more."
My mum smiles as a single teardrop taps the floor.

I asked, "If I were normal would you love me?"
Mum nodded, "Of course I would,
It doesn't matter what happens,
You're always my baby."
"I wanna be a superhero like you when I grow up."
I looked up at her with a soft stare.
She looked down and patted my head.
"You're already a superhero, my child."
She ruffled my hair.

My mum is a superhero, she is the best.
I'm her sidekick but when I grow up,
I'll be able to handle the rest.

Kai Beverton (15)

My Idol

My idol is my mum.
Always being there for me,
Seasons change with the beat of a drum,
So do we,
With our unwavering bond.

Many mums are quite lustrous,
But mine transcends beyond space.
She is vastly rustless!
As she is hard to displace.

Without her, life would be extraordinarily chaotic!
Showing support, from her pure angelic heart,
Exploring places, making her exotic!
If she departed, I would not be able to part.
Life, without my mum, would sting my heart.

I love her to the moon and back,
Not wanting her to change,
Nothing she does can ever lack!
Never exchanging her (even though she is strange).

You should always cherish loved ones,
As you never know when they will disappear.

Eleanor Lancaster (15)

My Majesty, My Queen

My majesty, my queen
Not even roses themselves can be as fragrant as her.
Her poses, glorious! You can't steal any of hers!
She speaks like she owns the crowns of all the world!
She spins like a talented ballerina,
Her voice echoes with the sumptuous breeze,
The whispers she utters are well on an arena!
The way her body poises with ease,
Like a contortionist, but with far more expertise!
That nourishing advice she declares in short,
They are so much better than an actual report.
Lots of freedom she'll resort,
I'd best not try and be dishonest,
For distrust, I don't want to be sought!
She has millions of harsh ways indeed,
Yet she follows her kindness so she will succeed,
The perfect woman for me.

Isra Butt (11)

My Hero

My hero doesn't wear a cape,
My hero isn't Superman or Wonder Woman,
My hero doesn't have super strength or the power to fly,
But she's the best friend I could ever ask for.

My hero and I have been friends for nine years,
And she never abandoned for other peers,
My best friend is really sweet,
I know she's better than the summer's heat.

When she moved schools I thought I'd never see her again,
But we became pals with a pen,
When we see each other I can't stop smiling,
All my cards keep piling and piling.

When we were young,
We had lots of fun,
At the My Little Pony movie,
We decided not to have a smoothie,
Iris is my best friend,
All the way to the end.

Mimi Clarke (14)

My Special Person

You're a star in the sky,
My cherry on top,
The breeze in my hair,
An iridescent raindrop.

Your smile illuminates my heart,
Your eyes are the light in the dark,
As radiant as the sun,
My electric spark.

You're a bubble of happiness,
That can never be burst,
You are astounding to be around,
This bubble can never fall to the ground.

You're my light, my dark,
The air I breathe,
You're my happiness,
The all that I need.

You're my lucky charm,
The reason my wishes come true,
My best friend,
Through and through.

You're a star in the sky,
My cherry on top,
The breeze in my hair,
But most of all,
You're my dad!

Ruby Cobb (12)

Something About Me

Am I ginger or am I blonde?
When people give comments I don't respond
My eyes, are they blue
Brown or grey too?

Myself happy or sad,
Elated or mad?
Who could care less
About me a little mess.

For I am me and me is I
And as a man I cannot cry.

My friends I have none
All the past friendships gone.
So I sit alone
Next to a garden gnome.

I go home last
It's all to do with my past.

But that was then
And now as they sit by my side
I know I am not lonely
It's how I bide.

I have a saying
Which has changed
It goes like this
About me who has changed.

I am me and me is I
I'm a man and I do not cry.

Aiden Wilson (12)

Remembrance

Smouldering clouds turned to red,
The sound of death returned,
Some soldiers climbed up ahead,
Whilst others were left to burn,
The rains of terror fell upon,
The soldiers and their cries,
It seemed all hope was gone,
And nothing was left but bitter lies.

Where holy brightness broke in flames,
And on the battlefield,
The memories and the corpses' names,
The rest were concealed,
The beach surrounded by ill-fated men,
All of them they had lost,
They fought and fought until then,
They had to pay the cost.

We will remember your sacrifice,
You made your country proud,
To be more concise,
You have stood out from the crowd,
You have given us the freedom to live,
And your losses we all deeply regret,
So this memorial to you we give,
Lest we forget.

Rameen Ali (14)

My Mom, My Hero

In a cosy home where love is always near,
A wearer of many hats, a friend so dear,
Mom's hugs wipe away my every tear.
Her voice, like music, calms every fear.

Mom's my sunshine on a cloudy day,
Her wisdom guides me in every way.
With her by my side, nothing's ever wrong,
In her embrace, I always feel strong.

When doubts arise, her love is my guide,
She's my superhero, with love spread wide.
A mentor, a friend, with inspiration's flame,
With her, life's journey is never the same.

So here's to Mom, the greatest of all,
Her love, a blanket, keeping me warm and tall.
Guiding me gently, each and every day,
Forever in my heart, her love will stay.

Aaditri Manjunath (10)

Superhero's Job

Flying through the city, looking down below,
Someone shouting, "I need a hero!"
Helping people is what I do,
If you need me I come to you.
This city has a hero,
That is me you know.
You can count on me
To help you, yes, me!
Police are jealous, I stole their job,
Setting up traps to get me locked up.
Firefighters taking fires,
But they're no match for my icy powers.
Plumbers fixing pipes,
But with super strength, I can do it overnight.
With my super vision I can find it in seconds,
People helped again with my superhuman powers.
If you need me again, I am out and about.
Just call me and shout!
I can help you at whatever time,
I will find you if you commit a crime.

Jude Meeks (13)

My Favourite Person

To love is truly an art
But sometimes we don't know where to start,
It can come from any direction,
Any aspect, any affection.
Love is kind and patient
Love is trustworthy but also ancient.
A feeling so strong,
Brings me and you along.
All else disappears,
Even erases some of my fears.
I feel at peace with you as you shall with me;
Crazy how it makes us feel like the world isn't even real,
Crosses all borders
Language, ethnicity and orders.
Time feels forgotten
Almost like it's untrodden.
Love can be found at any cafe
And I know this may sound a little cliché
But love is the best
And it comes from this little thing in my chest.

Oluwamomi Elugbaju (12)

My Mum

My mum is like a shining star,
A light that's always near or far.
She warms my heart with just her smile,
And makes each day feel so worthwhile.
She's there to catch me when I fall,
She listens when I need to call.
Her hugs are like a cosy nest,
In her embrace, I find my rest.
She teaches me with patient care,
To always love and always share.
Her wisdom guides me on my way,
She helps me grow more every day.
With every laugh and every tear,
She shows me that she's always here.
My mum's a treasure, pure and true,
I'm grateful for her love so blue.
So here's a thank you, dear and sweet,
For all the ways you make life neat.
My mum, my friend, my guiding light,
You make my world so warm and bright.

Abeerah Meher Saleem (12)

My Hero Is My Mum

My hero is...
My mum!
She is graceful,
She is bright,
She is a superhero,
She is smart like a genius,
She loves me and I love her too.

I love her!
She raised me and my siblings very well,
She takes care of the family,
She is helpful when I'm stuck on something that I don't know, she will help me.
That's why I love her and that's why she loves me too.

I will always support her like a pillar,
I will take care of her when she needs help.
I love my mum;
She is like a star to me.
She is like a sunflower.
She is like the sunshine.
My mum is an amazing woman,
She shapes my life and fills my heart with love.

David Chibundu Umensofor (9)

My Hero

She is facing challenges I could never face,
When the going gets tough she picks up the pace.
She lifts me up high and makes me laugh,
And yes, she has faltered in the past.

She is not alone in her troubles and strife,
There are others like her who plod through life.
I'm proud of her because she gets through the struggle,
And is always there to make me chuckle.

I see what a beautiful person she is growing up to be,
She is kind, caring, and full of creativity.
I love making her laugh and making her smile,
I haven't said this in a while.

My hero is the best person ever,
My little sister has ASD,
And I'll love her forever.

Eve Crutchley (12)

Clay

I don't know how to describe you,
Not kind or smart or free,
Because you're so much more than that,
At least more than that to me.

You are like my therapist,
Though you've struggled much yourself,
You stick with me through highs and lows,
Even though I should be giving you help.

To me you are a soldier,
Your whole life has been a war,
You're turning sixteen this year,
It's time to open up a new door.

Your friends are all behind you,
Supporting your every move,
You have nothing to be scared of,
We'll always be here for you.

Clay, my dear friend,
I love you to the moon,
You're still battling through so much,
And that's why I look up to you.

Eleanor Downey (12)

Joeboy

His music so sweet, like summer sunshine,
From Nigeria he hails, with talent divine,
In Afrobeat rhythms, his songs entwine.

Joeboy's voice, a magical spell,
In melodies and lyrics, he excels,
Bringing joy to hearts, in musical wells,
His tunes, like stories, he artfully tells.

In the realm of music, he's a shining star,
With each song, he elevates us far,
Joeboy's artistry, like a guiding spar,
In the world of sounds, he's set the bar.

So here's to Joeboy, with applause and cheer,
His music surrounds us, crystal clear,
In the realm of rhythm, he holds dear,
A maestro of melodies, without a peer.

Bright Adebowale (13)

A Journey Of Resilience

My mother, hero, left at nineteen years,
Escaping war, her past marked by her tears.
Through Guinea's plains and Senegal's harsh lands,
She faced her trials with strong, unwavering hands.

In England's shores, with sister by her side,
A land of hope, though fear she could not hide.
Through college halls and university,
She studied law with great tenacity.

She graduated, Master's in her hand,
She built our future with a steady hand.
A single mother, strength within her grace,
Her love and guidance, always in their place.

Her journey's marked by trials overcome,
My mother, hero, strong as she has become.

Joel Davies (17)

A Hero In My Eyes

The age of thirty-five brought him a fright,
One so big that it would make anybody despair at first sight,
But not he as it brought him an enemy to fight,
Thirty years... the war charges on but he thrives,
Accepting a foreign organ to stay alive,
But, setbacks must arrive as there would be no one resolution,
No one moment of relief,
Meds renew a binding contract that clings him to life,
His struggles set a flickering fire into light once again,
A burning reminder that anything is possible with determination,
compassion and a will to carry on the fight,
His love passed down to his son and then to me,
His accomplishments tell a story meant to inspire anyone in fighting their own battle in life.

Mohammed Lehry (14)

My Grandma

My grandma,
With paintbrush in hand,
Humming in the sunlight,
As she continues to paint
Her own view of the world.

Never letting us call her Granny,
With her five chickens and a cat,
She continues to wear her pleated skirts,
Colourful scarves and her summer hats.

There she is, baking her famous recipe:
Chocolate cupcakes with choc chips inside.

She always manages to make me smile
As soon as I enter the door,
Taking off shoes to pad across the cold kitchen floor.

Every room is filled with the smell
Of cupcakes and tea,
And her amazing paintings hanging up,
Which always inspire me.

Megan Munro (13)

The Dutch Man

I watch the world outside,
As one thought comes to mind,
The feeling of the touch,
Only the time I can trust.
Football calls his name,
Engulfed in all the fame,
The one who got it right,
Who I think about every night,
My one and true insight,
Is Virgil van Dijk.

From the numbers to the fans,
It never gets old,
It's always the Dutch Man,
Who stops all the goals,
Whether it's grass or sand,
It stays in my soul.
As clear as sky or as dark as coal,
An easy path,
Like cloth to ignite,
Or a hard path,
Like a carrot to bite!
Ignore the fight,
And listen, to Virgil van Dijk.

Reuben Mustoe (12)

Try Everything

You can do anything if you try,
You can hear the calls from the sky,
And you can even fly into the air so high.

You can feel the spirit so bright,
You can feel it oh so tight,
You can find your light,
Or gain might.

You can feel so shy,
You can start to cry,
But it's all part of life,
So you've got to try.

There is time to do it still,
You can try to find your skill,
You can rest and chill,
But there's time to do it still.

You've got to try for so long,
You've got to still be strong,
But the last thing to know is,
You're right, not wrong.

Maya Kasmani (9)

My Dad

Likes an adventure,
Likes a task,
Sometimes breaks the occasional glass.

Wrote a book,
Take a look.
He is clever,
Throughout all weathers.

Can run a mile or ten,
But not to London or Big Ben.
Loves to run more than most,
Especially along the coast.

Perseveres when a task is near.
Sometimes makes mistakes,
But dedicates,
To make whatever he wants to make.

Does a dance
And a prance.
This makes us laugh,
And we join in,
With a spin.

You will find
He's very kind.
So much fun we have,
These are my favourite things about my dad.

Lily Simpson (12)

Villain

You saved me.
I needed saving,
And you came.

I looked up to you,
Your beauty,
Your smile.
You showed me someone cared.

You were my hero.
But it's not like that anymore.

You left me,
All alone.
You took my friends,
My happiness.

You tell people how I hurt you.
How I am bad.
How I am toxic.
How I am the villain.

But maybe it's not me.
Maybe all I ever did was care about you.
And maybe all I ever wanted was for us to be the heroes in our story.

At least you were meant to be mine.
But you're not.
You are my villain.

Matilda Brown (14)

Heroines' Touch

Resounding *J.K. Rowling*,
Books about wizarding,

Hooks on the pillow, like an owl,
When I feel the shadows cowering,
in with the spell.

Smells like sweet Victoria sponge and traybakes,
That culinary *Mary Berry* makes.

For a role model,
and doyenne.

When I watch her cooking,
I feel zen.

The heroines' play-pen, like cleavers, healing.
They are all teaching, writing, leading,

Banners for manners, and,
Planters and planners.

They taste victory,
by remaining a mystery.

Heroines are now part of, her and,
our history.

Rosalind Thornhill-King (12)

My Hero

B ringing the joy to my world,
E very day I admire him,
S torms and chaos could have unfurled,
T hrough it, he would still be there with a grin.

D ad, you're so hardworking and you never stop,
A ll the time you're there to make sure I don't flop,
D ad, you are the one who keeps my spirits at the top.

E nter in a room with him he'll make you groan or laugh,
V ery bad are jokes from him but that is just his path,
E ven if you aren't amused he has some kind of charm,
R eady for just anything, he'll keep you out of harm.

Jude Quail (13)

Teacher, Teacher

Teacher, teacher,
You are my inspiration,
Without you, there would be no generation,
With your endless support, and your endless care,
You have built my attractive glare.
Thank you for the time you gave me,
Without it, I would not be free,
You honestly did shape society,
Words can't explain how amazing you are,
Besides the fact that you are a star,
And I know at times it can be tough,
But I want to let you know, the road is never rough,
When all you do is climb,
So I want to take this time,
To write this rhyme,
For every teacher around the world,
To tell them just how much they shine.

Gurneet Singh (13)

My Amazing Teacher

I admire my teacher
Because she's very beautiful, smart and funny.
She's a great and independent woman
Who doesn't take nonsense from anyone
And she is also very intelligent.

She's really hilarious
And loves all her students equally,
She's my favourite teacher
And really generous.
Whenever I feel upset,
She knows exactly what to say
To brighten up my smile.

I love my lovely, pretty, kind teachers equally.
My other teacher is as intelligent as my other teacher.
They both are very unique
And whenever they walk past me,
I can smell their special fragrance.

Alisha Ahmed (10)

Peace And Justice

On the battlefield, courage shines bright,
Soldiers march on with their might.
Through the chaos and strife,
They fight for love and life.

Bullets fly, bombs explode,
Yet their spirits will never erode.
They stand tall, united as one,
From freedom's cause, they won't be undone.

In the trenches, they find strength,
Bound by honour, they go to any length.
Their sacrifice, a noble deed,
For peace and justice, they bleed.

Though war brings pain and sorrow,
Their bravery shines through tomorrow.
We honour those who fought so bravely,
Their legacy, forever engraved.

Connie Edwards (12)

Taylor Thirteen!

T aylor Swift made me more confident when singing,
H er most popular songs inspired me to relate to her songs.
I think she brings me joy and lots of entertainment.
R ight now she has made eleven albums, with different stories,
T hough she is famous she records backstage and talks as if she's normal.
E vermore, one of her album names, relaxes me when I try to focus.
E ventually, as my music taste moved, her beat is what I want to repeat.
N ow you see the joy she made, following not what others want, but what she wants,

Her fans are real and I am one of them.

Emily Barrett (11)

The Best Brother Ever

I have a brother, his name is Tamjeed,
He is able to fulfil all of your needs.
He can calculate maths, jump up high,
And eat chocolate every day and night.

His hair is black, like a top hat,
And his eyes are dark brown, I'll give you that.
He has a cheeky smile made of soft rose lips,
And one of his favourite foods is chips.

We go together to ride our bikes,
And Nutella is something he really likes.
Together we can play video games,
Without him, my life would not be the same.

He has a special place in my heart,
And he is clever and really smart.
He will be here whenever I need,
And in life, he will always succeed.

Tahmeed Rahman (13)

My Hero

Who is my hero?
My dad is my hero
He is my friend, role model and inspiration
He is the one who guides and protects us
I feel safe every time in my dad's hands
He has taught me many valuable lessons
Through his sacrifices to provide for the family.

Through this, I have learnt to be brave, courageous
And believe in my capabilities.
His sacrifices are a source of motivation
Including our daily conversations to and from school.

He is irreplaceable and without him, I would struggle
My dad is the best, I love him, he is my treasure
And will always remain my number one hero.

Joyleen Shasha (8)

Harmony Of Friendship

In this friendship, our hearts do swoon,
If you laugh like the sun,
I smile like the moon.

Together we leap, in sync we groove,
If you jump up like a frog,
I bounce like a kangaroo.

Your words, a melody, a beautiful tune,
If you talk like a bird,
I listen like a butterfly.

In your joy, my spirits balloon,
If you are happy like a flower,
I am happy like a firework too.

In harmony, we move in our festoon,
If you dance like a crane,
I dance like a peacock.

For you, my friend, I'll always attune,
Say hello to my best friend,
You are the most understanding of me in the world!

Cotty Vicary (10)

My Mother

My mother helps me
With loads and loads and loads of things.
No matter how big, no matter how small,
She helps to lift me up when I fall.
When I was little she'd wipe my dirty bum,
So there's no way she isn't the best mum.
Now we've listed all the facts,
We listed this, we listed that,
So that's why she's my superhero!
It's been like that since I was zero.
She is my queen, my friend and also my mum,
And together we have loads of fun.
So now you see she's not just my mum,
She's my superhero and without her nothing's fun.

Zahara Lewis-Coombs (9)

My Best Friend: CG

Catrin is my best friend,
Our friendship will never end,
Her hair's so blonde and bright,
We chat until day becomes night,
We are always together,
No matter the weather,
We are with each other through thick and thin,
She is like my long-lost twin.

It was on Halloween,
We were only thirteen,
All so scared,
We weren't prepared,
We went to Gwyrch Castle,
Oh what a hassle,
Clowns jumping out,
Dragging people about,
Catrin stands by my side,
We will never divide,
We have grown up together,
And will carry on forever.

Alicia Jones (14)

The Little Glass Bells

Once in my dream,
I heard something true,
So pure and firm,
Glass bells silently proud,
Each ringing its little tune.

The little bells rang,
Faster each time,
Desperate times called,
But they were not weary.

They were positive,
And social at least,
But suffered great loss,
Trying to fill the hole in their heart.

Suddenly too soon,
I woke up abruptly,
Thinking about the harmonious tune,
But there is one more question,
One I did not ask.

Who were the glass bells
That sang to cure melancholy?

Hansikaa Mallieswaran (9)

My Teachers

Mysterious, captivating, tender
My teachers.

    M ajestic
    R espectful.

    C ourageous
    O utstanding
    R eliable
    L uxurious
    E nthusiastic
    T houghtful
    T alented.

Marvellous, considering, triumphant
My teachers.

    M odest
    R emarkable
    S uccessful.

T rustworthy
A ngelic
T hriving
T hankful
L oyal
E xquisite
R adiant.

Magnificent, champion, tender
My teachers.

Marzia Husseini (11)

The Story About My Loving Dad

My hero is my dad,
The most loving dad in the world in my opinion.
If I got hurt when I was younger,
My dad would be there if I got hurt
And my dad was always there
If I needed him when I was younger.
My dad taught me how to defend myself
And he also taught me how to fix a bike
And the gears of a manual car.
The best memory I have
Is when we went to the Isle of Man
And watched motorbike racing together
And had a laugh.
We also adventured at the Isle of Man.
I love my dad with all my heart,
That's why he's my hero.
My dad.

Macauley Heath Ward (14)

How They Plant The Seeds

Rain trickling down her face,
Like tears,
But only ever tears of joy she shed,
A constant jovial smile,
The flicker of green embers darting in her eyes,
Pale phoenix locks and golden ribbons,
How could a shadow be so unreal?
Sunlight mirroring the love of the morning sky.
How could a shadow be so unreal?
How is this to be?
Who lit a light?
One day,
Maybe soon,
Or maybe far,
Someday I will be the hero,
For others,
And for me,
Showing the people who plant seeds,
How they changed the world.
How they plant the seeds.

Zea Windett (12)

My Cousin, Erin

My cousin, Erin, is my favourite person.
She is funny and makes me happy.
Sometimes she is yappy.
Sometimes she wants to slap me!

She plays football just like me
But she will never be better than me you see!
We always play Fortnite, FIFA and Minecraft,
When we play she acts daft.

I sometimes stay in her house
Or maybe just twice a year.
When I talk to her half the time she can't even hear.
We were in her house filled with fear,
After a doll magically disappeared.

That's why my cousin is my favourite person.

Eoghan Bradley (12)

My Parents

M y amazing parents are the best,
Y ou don't need to question it.

A mazing bravery,
M ind-blowing accuracy,
A chieving and affectionate,
Z estful and loving,
I ncredible skills,
N oble-minded,
G entle and glamorous.

P arents are the best,
A musing you every day,
R especting and caring for you,
E xcellent intelligence,
N ever-ending enjoyment,
T hey will *never* stop loving you,
S o, those are my heroes.

Eva Richards (10)

What Is A Sister?

What is a sister?
Someone who is there
When you are hurting
She picks you up
And dusts you off again.

What is a sister?
Someone who sees you are without a smile
And gives you one of hers
She gives you a hug too
One especially for you.

What is a sister?
Someone who stands by your side
And holds you up while you cry
When things don't go well
She helps you understand.

What is a sister?
A cherished friend for life
A sister by blood
Blood-related or half
My hero at heart.

Jade Owen (14)

Zendaya Is My Hero

Zendaya is my hero,
She made my anxiety levels go to zero.
She made me want to work hard to become an actress,
Instead of always lying on my mattress.

I love Zendaya Coleman,
She makes my heart feel golden.
She always puts a smile on my face,
And makes me feel safe.

She inspires me so much,
And creates a scene of beauty such.
Zendaya can do anything,
As well as the comfort she can bring.

I hope I can meet her some day,
Oh, I pray and pray.
Zendaya will be my hero always,
For days and days.

Khloe Ndjoli (14)

How Do I Know?

How am I meant to know
If it's my mum or brother?
It doesn't really show,
It stays wrapped up,
It stays undercover.

How am I meant to know
Who's my favourite person?
How am I meant to choose
Either way somebody has to lose.

How am I meant to know?
There's a line I've got to cross,
But there's a line I've got to toe.

It's hard to decide so I think I pick my dogs,
They're always there and they always truly care.
With them, all my stuff I would happily share.

Brodie Terry (16)

The Great Tim Watson

T imes are tough but he pushes through.
I n times of trouble, he is there.
M ost days he always gives joy to people.

W hen it's dark his light shines through.
A wesome is what he is every day.
T here is no one who doesn't like him (seriously, my mates are obsessed).
S ometimes he has bad days but that doesn't change the positivity he gives out.
O nly shows hospitality and kindness to all his customers.
N ever has he had a day where he hasn't done something positive.

Charlie Watson (14)

Mummy

She never gives up.
She gives me love when I need it.
Mummy is my superhero.
She helps me when I need it the most.
She helps me with booboos and takes the pain away.
She makes my favourite foods.
She buys me what I need and makes me feel like me again.
My mummy is my superhero.

Mum's my hero.
She helps me when I don't know.
She helps me when I get stuck.
She helps me when I get hurt or fall.
I love my mum and she loves me.
When I was little she took care of me all day.
My mum is my hero.

Khadija Razaq (7)

The People Who Fought For Us

The poppies were planted
The poppies grow
The poppies are there to remember the ones who go
So when you're sitting there thinking of what to do
Remember to think about the ones who died for you
With thanks to the people who fought for us
Two minutes' silence is not nearly enough
For the people who fought for us
Lives move on
People move on
But no one will forget the people who can't move on
So on the eleventh of November
At 11am
Remember to stop and think about
The people who fought for us.

Grace Gavin-Sommerville (14)

Thank You

My dear mother,
Thank you for all these years,
In which you were my mother,
But also a friendly shoulder,
On which I can complain of all evils.

I know I haven't always been obedient,
But after every argument we have,
I just want you to receive a hug from me,
Accepting it along with my honest apology.

Every hug of yours improves my days,
By showing me that your love for me is true,
And without even thinking about it,
I say with my hand on my heart,
That there is no one better than you!

Megi Gancheva (15)

My Favourite Person

My mom is the best mentor.
She gives me the best ideas
At the right time at the right place.
She never fails to impress me.

I look up to her every day
And value what she teaches me.
She is the best in my heart
No matter the circumstances.

Seeing how tough the world can be
Proper advice will always help.
She never disappoints me
When it is the most difficult.

She is my motivator
And helps me feel determined.
With her help I feel encouraged
Even in the toughest challenges.

Temilayo Adegbaju (11)

The Way Of Life

My mum is so caring, she is forever meek.
My dad loves me so much, he encourages me.
Tom Fletcher books make me want to read and read.
Rachel Renée Russell books make me feel like me.
Netball is my favourite sport.
But when they are not playing fair
I feel like taking them to court.

My best friend, Hannah, helps me in school.
But when we're in the class I feel nice and cool.

These people inspire me in my way of life.
And they will forever be with me
As I go on a journey to find my path.

Anjolaoluwa Deborah Ojeyemi (11)

A Heroic Story: Jann Mardenborough

He once was a gamer,
Now turned into a racer,
His dad felt very unimpressed,
Unlike all the rest.

He tried to prove him wrong,
But went a bit too far,
His racing was loved by all,
But yet didn't feel happy at all.

He took his fame for the worst,
He felt unhappy with his accomplishments,
He tried to prove to the world that he was the best,
But failed, almost.

No matter what, he kept going,
Started to try harder,
Not letting anything in his path,
Until he succeeded.

Tyler Roberts (13)

Comet And Lunar: My Kittens

M y cute heroes love me and I love them too,
Y ou will easily get them mixed up because they are twins!

H appily they play with each other and share their toys,
E very day they wash each other to keep their coats sparkly white,
R acing around the house, they crash into everything!
O nly ten months old and they already feel like my best friends.
E very time they see us they purrrrrrrrr (they are right now!)
S weetly they sleep curled up together.

Miaow!

Hayley Aurora Yarwood (8)

My Little Brother

My poem is about my little brother,
He is four and he likes to roar
On the playroom floor
And it sounds very loud.
He has shiny green eyes
And he is smaller and a lot taller
Than people in his school.
He has dark blonde hair
Like a bear
And he is very cute but annoying.
When playing he finds it very funny.
He is always happy,
Especially when he eats his favourite food
Which is apples, bananas
And mint choc chip ice cream.
He is special to me because
He is kind, brave and adorable.

Evie Jones (11)

No Pain, No Gain

Striving to cater for her children
Until her last sweat drops.

As busy as a bee.
As loving as a mother.
In her embrace, I find my peace.
Her love and faith will never cease.

Making sure we are always at home.
But we are never alone.

She always tells me to learn hard
And let the sky be my limit.
Because if God be for us,
Who can be against us?

She always tells me that wherever you go,
Let your light shine.
Let it shine so bright,
That your foe will flee from you in seven.

Knowing how mighty you are.

Daniella Appiah (15)

Heroes Are...

- **H** eroic,
- **I** ntelligent,
- **D** ependable,
- **D** aring,
- **E** nergetic and
- **N** ever scared.

- **I** s what they all say,
- **N** ot...

- **P** olice officers,
- **L** awyers,
- **A** rtists,
- **I** nvestigators and
- **N** urses.

- **S** o what do you call a person who
- **I** s selfless and helps those in need.
- **G** oing out of their way for others.
- **H** eroes don't always wear a mask and cape,
- **T** hey're...

Yusra Taj (16)

The Man With A Story: My Grandad

With no food
And a wound
Rich and Bob Kinabalu escape
Covered in frost
Surrounded by apes
With no escape.

Travelling with his wife
Enjoying life
Going swimming in the water
With his granddaughter
With his grandson
Driving through London
Life couldn't get better.

Climbing with his son
The view stunned
Above the clouds
Sitting there for hours
Flowers blossomed everywhere
Devoured by the wind

My hero
One of a kind
My grandad.

Ailis Mayfield (13)

My Hero

My hero will always be there for me,
Even if we're at the bottom of the sea,
My hero loves me for who I am,
When I was little, he pushed me in my pram.

My hero makes me feel good,
He always makes sure I am clearly understood,
My hero makes sure I am well-fed,
He always tucks me into bed.

My hero always ensures I get the best experience,
People always say he is so hilarious,
My hero will never leave me,
With most of my opinions, he will agree.

My hero is my dad.

Juliet Else (11)

Bitter/Sweet

You walk in squares,
No thought, no reason;
The criticisms through which
The lens is warped.

I can tell it is there and
I try, in vain, although sometimes
Almost, to capture it;
The thing - the very
Concept unknown.

Circles in circles,
Ever spiralling in,
Pointing half-heartedly
To the precipice, the point,
The meaningless nothing that awaits -

And yet...

I know what I have felt,
It is slightly askew -
And until the day when words
At last mean no more
Yours will be those which I ever strive for.

Poppy Orr (17)

The Gods For One And All

Behold our saviours
A navy of sailors
An army of soldiers
An air force of warriors.

With every fight
They bring hope and light
Demolishing fear
They always persevere.

Here to defend
Their bravery has no end
Make your life worth their pain
Don't let their courage go in vain.

Thus may their story end slow or fast
Their greatness becomes the glorious past
And as their hearts for the country will never fall
They become the gods for one and all.

Meghana Meda (14)

Erling Haaland

When times are tough, he makes me happy.
From strong Norway to the yellow Dortmund,
Then to the mighty blue Manchester.
Smashing the Prem goal record
And getting robbed by Messi in the Ballon d'Or.
Proving he's the best youngster in the world in his debut season.
He's as tall as a tree, as high as aiming for the treble.
He's built like an unstable robot.
He's never let me down.
Helping Man City win the Champions League.
The mighty Erling Haaland is in town!

Luca Faulkner (13)

My Gran-Tastic Hero

My granny is...
An ice cream licker,
A pancake creator,
A vegetable gobbler,
She's a food-loving hero.

My granny is...
A law enforcer,
A badminton player,
A criminal catcher,
She's an action superhero.

My granny is...
A Chinese speaker,
An English learner,
A try-something-newer,
She's a young at heart hero.

My granny is...
A game player,
A laugh maker,
A story weaver,
She's my gran-tastic hero.

Olivia Hollinworth (8)

To PB

My hero is PB,
No, not peanut butter.
She's got brown, thick hair up to her shoulders
And bright blue eyes.
When she smiles it fills me with joy,
Her loud laugh makes me giggle.
When times are tough she reassures,
She's there for me like a cuddly bear.
My favourite memory is when we were in Disneyland Paris,
Having a blast
On to Space Mountain where we got stuck,
We laughed for days like nothing else.
To PB,
I love you more than peanut butter on toast.

Tia Hurt-Field (14)

Milo

M   y tail twitches as I walk around the lonely house,
I   can hear them coming! Or was that a mouse?
L   icking them to make sure they are clean.
O   h! *Raff raff!* I must be seen!

I'm Milo, people say I am a little boy,
But I am actually really scary! Ask my toy.
I'm Milo, at home I am the king of the world,
But when I go outside I am scared of just a bird.
The point is, I am not just a dog with cute looks;
I am smart too, that is why I tear up your textbooks!

Stella Rajkumar (14)

Kohli, The Unstoppable Hero

Kohli, Kohli, Kohli
Phenomenally smashing
Nobody can match his confidence
He is invincible
A run machine
His teammates are thankful he is there
He always saves the day!

Kohli, Kohli, Kohli
Never can be stopped
He always keeps his cool
Always exercising every day
Not lying in a swimming pool!

Kohli, Kohli, Kohli
He is the best in every format
No one can beat him
Bowl any speed to him
He will smash it out of the cricket stadium!

Ayan Varma (9)

Lucas Akins

Lucas Akins running down the wing
It makes the Mansfield supporters sing
Lucas Akins is the best
If he left Mansfield I would be depressed
He takes Mansfield to win the cup
We all sing, we're going up
When he starts to advance
The Mansfield fans start the chants
Mansfield Town have won the league
Lucas Akins is a scoring machine
Lucas Akins, he shines so bright
We will celebrate and sing all night
You always know what to do
Akins, Akins, we love you.

James Short (14)

My Nanna

My hero is my nanna,
She has looked after me since I was nearly three.
She has given me a loving home, takes care of me.
Takes me on holiday to caravan parks,
Where I have so much fun.
We have lots of laughter and so much fun.
My hobbies are karate and basketball,
Playing games where my nanna has encouraged me,
She supports me in everything that I do.
I love school and my favourite subject is maths.
I wouldn't be the person I am today if it wasn't for my nanna.

Daniel Kiley (9)

My Favourite Person

My favourite person is my little sister, Aksara.
She is my favourite person because she understands me.
I enjoy it when she accompanies me.
I love playing with her as she makes up cool and fun games.
Me and my family enjoy her talking and her activities.
I am so proud of her coming into my life.
She is fun, creative and super sweet at hugging.
I've enjoyed watching her grow up since she was a baby.
I am so lucky to have a sister like her.
I will love her forever!

Adhisaya Nagulenthiran (10)

Dear Best Friend

In life's journey, a friend so dear,
Brings laughter, wipes every tear.
Through highs and lows, they stand by your side,
In their presence, joy and love abide.

With words of wisdom, they light your way,
In their embrace, troubles sway.
Their loyalty, a treasure so rare,
In their friendship, none can compare.

So raise a toast to your best friend true,
In their company, skies are always blue.
Cherish the bond that time can't sever,
For in your best friend, you find forever.

Tiarna Forbes (15)

Harry Styles

This place has no fate, no breath
Who determines who is ill and who is healthy?
If you find your favourite playlist to listen to each day
To and from your job
Maybe it would be you behind the partition
The playlist I make for myself
Gives me three weeks more health
Than the three weeks I spent inside of you
You
Lesbionic rage never touched you
We were like crossed hands
In the Harry Styles music video
That I never loved you enough to show you.

Khudeeja Begum (18)

Amy Winehouse

From her eyes lined with wings to her strong accent,
Her dark raven hair pulled up into tall updos,
Her wondrous voice dances through our ears,
Singing 'Back to Black' then jumping to upbeat vocals,
Yet sadly all songs must end,
Though her voice still plays through our minds,
And her timeless songs in our hearts forever,
Never forgotten.
Remembered for her voice, hair, looks, talents,
And the wonderful joy her voice brought to this dull world.

Lily Parkin (13)

Enid Blyton

E xciting books that she writes
N ovels full of fun and surprises
I nspiring readers as far as she can reach
D eeply touching every creative soul.

B right endings all her books have
L ively stories that never end
Y oung publisher as successful as she could achieve
T alented yet hardworking
O pening a new book filled to the brim with adventures
N ever did Enid Blyton give up her dream.

Caroline Deng (9)

Thirteen's The Luckiest Number

You can count me with the Potter fans
For making him did not go quite to plan
There was a slight hiccup in J.K.'s operation
Twelve companies denied her publication!
But the thirteenth happily found not one single flaw
So Harry was met with roaring applause!
To be able to be pushed so far down and zoom right back up
Is the kind of person that I want to become
Resilient, brave and never backed out
Rowling wins for me, without a doubt.

Daisy Stockford (11)

Oscar

My friend Oscar is as funny as a clown,
My friend Oscar turns my frown upside down.
My friend Oscar is as good at rugby as a pro,
My friend Oscar is the greatest person I know.
My friend Oscar's smile stretches from ear to ear,
My friend Oscar has no fear.
My friend Oscar is the smartest in my class,
If I have a question I know who to ask.
My friend Oscar is a good friend and always has been,
I'm lucky to have a friend like him!

Elliott Street (9)

My Hero, Meg

M e and you are meant to be,
Y ou make me laugh when I'm empty.

H ellos and goodbyes can make memories,
E ven through centuries.
R ough times happen but you make me smile,
O ver that time I think, *you made my trial*.

M eg, you don't know how special you are.
E very day I say, "Hey Meg, I love you,"
G ive me a hug and that's a dream come true.

Maisy Williams (12)

My Granny

My granny is a hero,
My granny is a friend,
My love for her is like a song,
That will never ever end.

Oh, let me feel her hug,
And hear her wise true words,
I feel admiration inside,
Like little, fluttering birds.

If I call her I need time,
We'll spend too long together,
She's my true inspiration,
The perfect grandmother.

Always there when I need her,
A strong, a calm support,
My love, it fizzes for her,
My favourite, calm resort.

Lydia Joy (12)

My Kind Of Friend

- **F** unny, someone equivalent to a sunny day
- **R** eliable, someone who can be trusted and won't ever go away
- **I** ntrepid, someone willing to be brave when you can't be
- **E** mpathetic, someone who is there for you through the good and bad
- **N** oble, someone who doesn't belittle or hurt people and honours honesty above all else
- **D** edicated, someone who always has time for your needs.

That is a good friend.

Alae Habbal (10)

Our Number Twenty-Six

He may be Scottish but we all know he's Scouse.
He came unknown, now he's a stern part of our house.
His football abilities are great, from tackles to crosses.
Andrew Robertson pockets people like he's one of the bosses.
His jokes fill joy in many faces.
His passes are precise in all places.
If he were to leave, it would fill Liverpool fans with sorrow.
His best moments proceed to fill minds yesterday, today and tomorrow.

Logan Jones (13)

My Heroes

My dad,
Who is never sad.
My grandma,
Who is like a star.
My grandad,
Who is always in a car
Is one of my stars.
My grandma and grandad who love tea
As well as me.
My brothers,
Who tease me constantly.
My mum,
Who I love.
My dog,
Who steals my food
And hides
Of greed.
My friends,
Who have hope.
These are my heroes,
Who stand tall and high,
Like stars in the sky.

Sofia Dingsdale-Rasburn (10)

My Hero

My hero is my mummy.
We skip to the cinema to watch our favourite movies.
We always make happy memories.
I love going to the toy store to get my favourite toy,
Which brings me so much joy.
Me and my mummy laugh and joke together.
My mummy is always there for me when I need her.
My mummy is my queen.
Every day is like a dream.
My mummy shows me the way.
I wish to be like my mummy one day.
I love my mummy.

Ariana Iqbal (7)

Mum Is A Hero!

    M um, you are too kind,
yo **U** have a creative mind!
    M um, you show too much love, you are as sweet as the sky above.

    I think you are as sweet as a dove,
  "S he's lovely!" everyone declares.

    T rue, it's a fact, she never scares,
    H er true love is just too sweet!
    E very word is a steady beat...

Mum, you are the...
Best!

Ezinne Ronami Turner (8)

Mum

My hero is my mum,
She is just loads of fun!
She's the one who cooks for me,
She's the one who looks after me.

Every morning she wakes me up,
Every day she treats me like a pup.
After school, I come back exhausted,
I see her and realise I feel supported.

When it is dark at night,
She tucks me in and turns off the light.
Now it is morning again,
I hope this never ever ends.

Shayna Pancholi (10)

A Woman So Pretty

Did you ever see a woman so pretty?
Walking around Brighton city?
The wind blowing through her hair,
The sun making the colour look ever so fair.

My favourite person,
Always longing to see,
Always meaning so much,
To someone like me.

Cherishing the moments we shared,
But always wishing you were still there,
Even if we are apart,
Forever holding our memories in my heart.

Allie Wolloff (15)

My Mother

She is mine, always mine
She is kind, always kind
She's my first friend, she's my first teacher
Who gives me the correct path to move further
She can be angry sometimes, wrong
Though or not, a loveable one
She cooks, cleans, and clatters
A helping hand, always her
A hard-working person, always her
She's everyone's hero
She is my beloved, my mother
And I love her.

Shaswi Agrawal (12)

My Favourite Person

My beautiful nephew
He is like a shining star in the sky
As soon as I saw him
My heart just melted.

He gets stronger every day
He is my little ray of sunshine
And he also has lots of hair
He is the cutest baby I know.

I really appreciate him
I am grateful for him, always and forever
I really wish I could have him forever
His name is Cillian, and he's all mine.

Faith Varndell (13)

Mum

My hero is my mum,
She puts yummy food in my tum.
When I feel sad,
She makes me glad.
She tickles my belly,
Until I laugh like jelly.

My mummy is very kind,
And she always reads my mind.
If I am feeling gloomy,
She always sings silly songs to me.

Whenever I get hurt,
My mummy gives me a dessert.
I love her very much,
Because she has a gentle touch.

Kaylen Pancholi (7)

My Hero, My Mom

My mum,
What is the definition of my mum?
There isn't any.
There are no words I can describe my mum with.
I can't describe my mum but I can say one word for her.
Amazing.
My mum is the best person in the world,
A person who can take care of me no matter what happens.
I am my mum's everything and I can't ask for anything from God because I have the most valuable person in the world, my mum.

Nandini Singh (11)

Let Me Describe My Favourite Person

My favourite person cares for me.
She helps me when times are rough.
If she wasn't here, I would have never existed.
The person I am writing about is obviously my mother.
Even if she's too busy at work, she still finds time for me.
She has been with me for the majority of my life.
She is good-hearted, and gives me good examples.
She gives me advice as I go to secondary school.

Victor Umahi Ndiwe (11)

He Is My Hero

He makes me happy when I am sad
He is my hero, he is my dad
He always finds good in my bad
He is my hero, he is my dad
I always look for him around
When he calls my name in a lovely sound
The happiness just has to add
He is my hero, he is my dad
For me to become successful
He is always kind and helpful
I want him to be proud and glad
He is my hero, he is my dad.

Hateem Safdar (12)

My Best Friend

Alice is my best friend,
I admire her because she has always been there for me,
I have known her for years,
She is funny, makes me laugh all the time,
Helpful, helps me when I am upset and
When I need help with work,
Kind, she is kind to me all the time and caring,
Ginger hair, with blue eyes,
And a little bit taller than me,
This is why I am inspired by my best friend.

Emily Rowlands (13)

Love About My Mum

M y mummy is not just a hero, she's a special hero.
Y ou would be happy if you had a mummy like mine.
H uge hugs are amazing from my magnificent mummy.
E ven if I'm feeling super sad, my mummy will always make me happy.
R elaxing on the sofa is a thing that me and Mummy do together.
O nly my mummy does the best things in my happy life.

Enzo Tavaglione (6)

My Hero Is...

Many people idolise famous people that they will likely never meet. Not me.
My hero is my mum!
She's been in pain for over a year, yet she still gets on with her life.
She gives me the best life that she can provide for me, and all the love in her heart.
She has her flaws, imperfections and insecurities, she doesn't pretend to be perfect.
I love my mum.
My mum loves me.

Amelia Wagstaff (12)

Aaliyah Crossley

She has brown hair,
Like a grizzly bear,
Who breathes air,
And wears purple glasses,
To see the world,
With her lashes,
She stops the dust,
From blinding her,
That brain of hers,
So crazy and kind,
She can't stop being so funny,
That would make her a dummy,
I am so lucky,
That she is my friend,
And I hope we shall always be friends.

Matylda Firth (12)

Sister

My older sister is a sea of flowers,
Her aroma travels all around,
She is as soft as tulips,
Yet can prick like a rose.
I see a picturesque mirror when I look at her,
Her luscious curls dancing in tune with the sun,
Her everlasting kindness sings a silent song,
Her majestic eyes see only angels in a world of devils.
But most of all I see
A lifelong best friend.

Amber Da Silva Lima (12)

Poetry Idol

She is always there
To support me when I am lonely.
She is always there
To cheer me up when I am sad.
She is always there
To make me correct when I am wrong.
She is always there
To help me when I am in trouble.
She is always there
To boost my confidence when I am nervous.
So that's the reason why
She is my idol.
My idol is...
My mum.

Abheer Shetty (11)

Thrill Of This Sport

F or every race
O nly unknown once
R ed flags, yellow flags and pit stops in-between
U plifted fans who are keen
M ay only be live once
L ucky drivers taking pole positions
A nd home races

O nly Formula One
N o race could be predicted
E verlasting thrills of Formula One with more to come.

Lydia Difford (11)

My Teacher Who Inspires Me

T his is the person who I admire
E ach day I aspire to be more like her
A nd her way of teaching is very enjoyable and interesting
C hatting to her cheers me up and lifts my emotions
H er personality is very calm and cheery
E very day, seeing her lightens my day
R eading, writing, having time with her will be memorable.

Khadija Rehman (10)

Tree

You were and are my roots,
My past that will follow me to my future.
You watched me grow,
Bloom like a blossom.
My family so deep within me,
You unlock me with your key.
How you grew me up and led me
So we wouldn't be apart.
Just know I will love you with all my heart.
You are the light I need to grow,
And I will make sure you know.

Ellie Hewitt (15)

My Little Hero

When I'm feeling down
We pick each other up and
We swirl each other around
I love her so much
We give each other
The warmest hugs ever
She plays with me when I am sad
That makes me so glad
She's by my side
She's the best anyone could ask for
So I say
She's the best sister
In the world!
I love her so much.

Grace Ilupeju (10)

My True Hero

My true hero is lovely.
My true hero is a delight.
She is so sweet
And so kind too.
She is a wonderful chef
And a lovely person too.
My mother is so sweet and kind,
Just like a cake.

My mother is so sweet,
Like ice cream.
She is a lovely mother
And a kind one too.
I love my mother,
Just as I love my dad too.

Mrinal Shrestha (11)

My Kind-Hearted Hero

My kind-hearted hero
Through good times and bad
She is the glue to hold us together
When we are sad.

She is the light at the end of my tunnel
I dream to be half as strong as her
Oh to be the wonderful, amazing woman she is
I hope one day to be just like her
So cheers to my beautiful mummy
That I love and care for so much.

Cora O'Hagan (13)

A Singular Blue Rose

I look for you in crowds I drown in
Fingers looped in the worn-down
Battered straps of my bag
My lifeline
Replacing the sweaty warmth
Of fingers I adore to hold
Which slip away
Without fail
Leaving my hands cold - and holding
So much tighter to those haggard bag straps
Losing grasp of that fleeting warmth
And hope.

Vida Lukas (15)

They're Not Just My Parents, They're My Friends Too!

She is kind and loving
She is a mother of two.

She works hard at a bar.
She's not just a mother,
She is my friend too.

He is kind and loving
Just like her.
He works as hard as he can.
He loves and loves.

His two children and his wife too.
He's not just a father,
He is a friend too.

Emma Williams (12)

Garnacho

Chipped on a wire, fell into a fire
That's why he's on fire, by scoring loads of goals
Bud-um-bum-bum
No one is faster than him
So there's no point in challenging him
Garnacho, Garnacho
Don't
Even
Think
About
Challenging
Him
Garnacho.

Garnacho! Kapow! Yeah!

Henry Fattorusso (9)

My Number One

My mum, my hero,
Through thick and thin.
She's always been there,
Her love and strength is beyond compare.
I dream to be half as amazing as her,
She is filled with so much care.
She is always lifting the mood in the air,
So here's to my mum, my number one,
I am forever grateful for all that she has done.

Anna Lean (13)

My Hero, My Mum

My mother is my hero, and there's no arguing with that.
She loves me overwhelmingly and I love her back.
She always has understood me and helped me grow.
After all, she's there for me, and that I know.
And yet still she stands there at our front door,
Ready to welcome me after a long day of school...

Amy Best (12)

My Mum

My mum is my hero and this is why...
She is kind
She is caring
She is independent
She is selfless
She is loving
She is always willing to speak her mind
She is always there for you no matter rain or shine
She is a real definition of a super good mum
And there are just a few reasons why.

Gracey-Ellen Bestwick (11)

Salah: My Football Hero

M y prayer is to know you
O n the pitch a crazy banger

S uper fast and courageous you go
A minute in, you've already scored
L egends out there who make role models so do you
A trip to see you is a dream come true
H ero forever, today and tomorrow.

Musa Alam (6)

The Best Of Armed Forces

The one who fights for our sins.
The one who flies to make us grin.
My auntie who marches along the road.
And the man who flies for Remembrance Day
To remember the lives of fallen men.
Ex-Typhoon pilot and ex-cadet Red 1 and my hero, Natalie Heap,
Stand side by side to make us smile.

Oliver Heap (13)

Mum

My favourite person is my mum,
She cooks food for me, yum!
Takes care of me when I'm sick
And kicks away the bad things.
Sings for me and reads for me,
Cleans for me and sits beside me.
Makes me my favourite tea.
Helps me with my homework too!
Shh! Even cleans my poo!

Avneet Kaur (8)

Formula For Love

My dad is A, my mum is B
The square root of them led to me, C.
Their love is sweeter than pi
And much more infinite.
The perimeter of my heart
Is the circumference of their love.
They help me see the world
Through the right angle.
Through their eyes
I'm acute.

Myriam Amin (8)

My Mom

My mom is a hero
My mom gives me kisses whilst I lie low on my pillow at night
My mom helps me surmount obstacles and challenges and I can always count on her
My mom inspires me, because she saves lives
My mom is love, because she's just so calm
My mom is my always and forever!

Charly Hecox (10)

My Dad

Big as an oak tree
Gives me a lot of hugs
He is my dad.

Brave as a honey badger
Good at growing plants
He is my dad.

Caring like an elephant
Great at gift-giving
He is my dad.

Draws like an artist
Has a cool haircut
He is my dad.

Yousuf Shah (8)

Hazel F

She is kind
She can do a cartwheel
She helps me
She takes me swimming
She tucks me up at bedtime
She looks after me
She shouts at me
She says sorry
She is the best writer
She reads to me
She bought me a dog
She doesn't like cleaning up her poo.

Blossom Fattorusso (6)

My Poem

When I'm in my room feeling down
She's always in town
She's my sister alright
The one with might
Never need to look for her
She's always by my side
She'll never leave me
She's mine!
She's a hero
I can never decline.

Joy Ilupeju (8)

My Parents, My Heroes

I love my parents the most
I love them both
My mom is the best
She is better than the rest
My dad cares for me
He is there to be
They take care of our family
Love my siblings, including me
I love my parents the most
I love them both!

Hareer Akram (9)

My Auntie

- **A** lways amazing, always kind
- **U** nique, probably the most unique person ever
- **N** ice and kind, loving and caring
- **T** eaches me many things
- **I** ncredibly important to me
- **E** legant, excellent, enjoyable, that's how she is.

Eshaal Zahid (10)

My Hero

I have a hero.
A helpful, strong and special one.
She loves me so much and I love her.
She gives me kisses and cuddles.
When I'm glum she comes and cheers me up with tickles and stories.
Do you know who she is?
It's my mummy!

Maggie Egerton (7)

Small

Frankie is cool
And he's a tad small
I lost him in the shop
Instead, I bought some Coco Pops
He's amazing at hide-and-seek
He's beat everyone there is to beat
I will see you in a while
Shopping in the kids' aisle.

Finley Stott (13)

My Hero Grandad

I love my grandad
He's the best
He's seventy-three
He likes doing gardening
Just like me
His favourite animal
Is a dog
He likes the colour yellow
And he loves cricket
I love my grandad
And he loves me.

Josie Robertson (9)

My Hero

I've never met my hero
But I will always look up to her.
I love her music!
It's my favourite type of music.
She's my idol
And I'm pretty sure I'll never stop loving her.
My idol is Taylor.
Taylor Swift.

Aycha Ben-Saïd (9)

Writers

W riting is a gift
R ewarding for the author
I n their own world
T here are no limits
E xcept their own imagination
R ead their books
S hare the story of a lifetime.

Ewan Jones (17)

Star

Happy dog.
Sleepy dog.
They're both cute.
Playful dog.
Daft dog.
Fun to have.
Lapdog.
Soft dog.
Good if you're a sleeper.
Coffee dog.
Food beggar dog.
Good if you like food.

Robin Brown (8)

My Brother

My brother is my glow.
He likes to go with the flow.
We are the unbreakable duo.
We used to play Lego but we grew.
He is the older Summers.
He is worth acres with no haters.
He is my brother and I love him.

Georgina Summers (12)

Shooting Star

Dancing around the galaxy
Partying around in my dazzling dress
Smaller stars feeling envy
Shiny sun showing up to the party
Smaller stars following me and the sun
Don't be scared, you will get there one day!

Vivienne Evette Georgieva (10)

Harrison The Swimmer: My Friend

Harrison Leonard
He has the brains
He can be good at other things
But he's better in the waves

Swimming can be hard
It makes no sense
Harrison's the opposite
He is swimming lengths.

Morgan McVicar (13)

My Mum

My mum is a creature from a world of teddies.
My mum is an angel from far away, or a bookshelf full of wisdom.
My mum is a suitcase with objects brimming with life.
My mum is a washing machine turning with joy.

Amelie Isenburg Daw (12)

My Sister

My sister makes me laugh, she calls me a chicken!
My sister is pretty, she looks like a princess.
She likes singing all the time.
She likes arts and crafts, just like me.
My sister is truly the best!

Rereloluwa Solaru (8)

TS

My inspiration is a funny, great friend.
He acts like a comedian,
But he looks like a chameleon.
He's funny but has no money.
He's a biker but crashes 'cause he's *hyper!*

Alfie Webbern (13)

Family

F riends to me always
A nd they are my heroes
M ore love every day
I n this group I am safe
L ike magic guardians they protect me
Y es, they are awesome!

Olivia Dodimead (9)

My Hero

In my world
You are my hero.
When I lose my way
You lead me.
When I'm hurt
You know that something is wrong.
When I need a life to lift me,
You have a heart to share.

Nicole Bujor (9)

My Mummy

- **M** y mum is the best
- **U** nique is what she helps me to be
- **M** ummy is my hero
- **M** akes lots of yummy things to eat
- **Y** eah, my mummy and me are lots of fun.

Tanvi Mishra (6)

My Hero: Daddy

Strong and has tattoos
Claps his hands for me when I achieve
Is the best dad in the world
Works hard to make me smile
Try your best
My hero, the best hero.

Heidi Colbert (10)

Daniel James

Daniel James is my inspiration
Likes kicking balls over the wall
Goes top bins and scores good balls
As fast as a sports car.

Joshua Marcou (12)

My Teacher Is My Hero

From Amina to Miss and all teachers

- **H** elpful
- **E** ncouraging
- **R** esponsive
- **O** nly awesome.

Amina Ali (5)

War Never Changes

A haiku

Ravaged lands still weep
History echoes the same
War's unchanging song.

Glen McBain (15)